THE MOST DANGEROUS GAME

and Other Stories of Adventure

THE MOST DANGEROUS GAME

and Other Stories of Adventure

DOVER THRIFT EDITIONS

Richard Connell, Jack London,
O. Henry, Clark Ashton Smith,
John Kruse and Rudyard Kipling

DOVER PUBLICATIONS
GARDEN CITY, NEW YORK

DOVER THRIFT EDITIONS

GENERAL EDITOR: SUSAN L. RATTINER
EDITOR OF THIS VOLUME: MICHAEL CROLAND

Bibliographical Note

The Most Dangerous Game and Other Stories of Adventure, first published by Dover Publications in 2021, is a new anthology of short stories reprinted from standard sources. Misspellings, minor inconsistencies, and other style vagaries derive from the original texts and have been retained for the sake of authenticity. A new introductory Note has been specially prepared for this edition.

Library of Congress Cataloging-in-Publication Data

Names: Connell, Richard Edward, 1893–1949, author. | London, Jack,
  1876–1916, author. | Henry, O., 1862–1910, author. | Smith, Clark Ashton,
  1893–1961, author. | Kruse, John, 1919– author. | Kipling, Rudyard,
  1865–1936, author.
Title: The most dangerous game and other stories of adventure / Richard
  Connell, Jack London, O. Henry, Clark Ashton Smith, John Kruse, and Rudyard
  Kipling.
Description: Garden City, New York : Dover Publications, 2021. | Series: Dover
  thrift editions | Summary: "Readers seeking exotic locales and nonstop
  pulse-pounding thrills will love this collection of six classic adventure
  stories"—Provided by publisher.
Identifiers: LCCN 2021000890 | ISBN 9780486848228 (trade paperback)
Subjects: LCSH: Adventure stories, American. | Adventure stories, English.
Classification: LCC PS648.A36 M67 2021 | DDC 813/.08708—dc23
LC record available at https://lccn.loc.gov/2021000890

Printed in the United States of America
84822103
www.doverpublications.com

Note

THIS COLLECTION OF classic adventure stories gives readers exotic locales and nonstop, pulse-pounding excitement.

Richard Connell's "The Most Dangerous Game" takes the thrill of hunting to an extreme conclusion, with human beings as the prey. It explores the nature of violence, the competing interests of society and the individual, and the ethics of hunting for sport. The first of two stories by Connell to win the O. Henry Memorial Award, "The Most Dangerous Game" has been frequently anthologized and studied in schools, and it inspired several film adaptations, with the original appearing in 1932. The story was published in *Collier's Weekly* on January 19, 1924.

Connell was a versatile and prolific writer. He began his career covering baseball for his father's *Poughkeepsie Press* at age ten, and he became the city editor at sixteen. He was the editor of Harvard's *The Crimson*, a journalist on the homicide desk for the *New York American*, and an advertising copywriter, and he edited a military publication, *The Gas Attack*, when he served in the Army during World War I. Connell penned more than 300 short stories, which were published in *The Saturday Evening Post*, *Collier's Weekly*, and many other American and English magazines. He wrote nonfiction magazine articles, four novels, and thirteen screenplays. The year after "The Most Dangerous Game" was published, he began a successful career as a scenario writer for major Hollywood studios.

This volume includes five other time-honored adventure stories. Jack London's "To Build a Fire" was published in *Century Magazine* in August 1908. O. Henry's "The Caballero's Way" appeared in his anthology *Heart of the West*, published by Doubleday, Page & Company in 1904. Clark Ashton Smith's "The Seed from the Sepulchre" was published in *Weird Tales* in October 1933. John Kruse's "Alone in Shark Waters" was published in *Collier's* on May 9, 1953. Rudyard Kipling's "The Man Who Would Be King" appeared in his collection *The Phantom 'Rickshaw & Other Eerie Tales*, published by A. H. Wheeler and Co. in 1888.

Contents

THE MOST DANGEROUS GAME

Richard Connell

"OFF THERE TO the right—somewhere—is a large island," said Whitney. "It's rather a mystery—"

"What island is it?" Rainsford asked.

"The old charts call it 'Ship-Trap Island,'" Whitney replied. "A suggestive name, isn't it? Sailors have a curious dread of the place. I don't know why. Some superstition—"

"Can't see it," remarked Rainsford, trying to peer through the dank tropical night that was palpable as it pressed its thick warm blackness in upon the yacht.

"You've good eyes," said Whitney, with a laugh, "and I've seen you pick off a moose moving in the brown fall bush at four hundred yards, but even you can't see four miles or so through a moonless Caribbean night."

"Nor four yards," admitted Rainsford. "Ugh! It's like moist black velvet."

"It will be light enough in Rio," promised Whitney. "We should make it in a few days. I hope the jaguar guns have come from Purdey's. We should have some good hunting up the Amazon. Great sport, hunting."

"The best sport in the world," agreed Rainsford.

"For the hunter," amended Whitney. "Not for the jaguar."

"Don't talk rot, Whitney," said Rainsford. "You're a big-game hunter, not a philosopher. Who cares how a jaguar feels?"

"Perhaps the jaguar does," observed Whitney.

"Bah! They've no understanding."

"Even so, I rather think they understand one thing—fear. The fear of pain and the fear of death."

1

"Nonsense," laughed Rainsford. "This hot weather is making you soft, Whitney. Be a realist. The world is made up of two classes—the hunters and the huntees. Luckily, you and I are hunters. Do you think we've passed that island yet?"

"I can't tell in the dark. I hope so."

"Why?" asked Rainsford.

"The place has a reputation—a bad one."

"Cannibals?" suggested Rainsford.

"Hardly. Even cannibals wouldn't live in such a God-forsaken place. But it's gotten into sailor lore, somehow. Didn't you notice that the crew's nerves seemed a bit jumpy today?"

"They were a bit strange, now you mention it. Even Captain Nielsen—"

"Yes, even that tough-minded old Swede, who'd go up to the devil himself and ask him for a light. Those fishy blue eyes held a look I never saw there before. All I could get out of him was 'This place has an evil name among seafaring men, sir.' Then he said to me, very gravely, 'Don't you feel anything?'—as if the air about us was actually poisonous. Now, you mustn't laugh when I tell you this—I did feel something like a sudden chill.

"There was no breeze. The sea was as flat as a plate-glass window. We were drawing near the island then. What I felt was a—a—mental chill; a sort of sudden dread."

"Pure imagination," said Rainsford. "One superstitious sailor can taint the whole ship's company with his fear."

"Maybe. But sometimes I think sailors have an extra sense that tells them when they are in danger. Sometimes I think evil is a tangible thing—with wave lengths, just as sound and light have. An evil place can, so to speak, broadcast vibrations of evil. Anyhow, I'm glad we're getting out of this zone. Well, I think I'll turn in now, Rainsford."

"I'm not sleepy," said Rainsford. "I'm going to smoke another pipe up on the afterdeck."

"Good night, then, Rainsford. See you at breakfast."

"Right. Good night, Whitney."

There was no sound in the night as Rainsford sat there but the muffled throb of the engine that drove the yacht swiftly through the darkness, and the swish and ripple of the wash of the propeller.

Rainsford, reclining in a steamer chair, indolently puffed on his favorite brier. The sensuous drowsiness of the night was on him. "It's so dark," he thought, "that I could sleep without closing my eyes; the night would be my eyelids—"

An abrupt sound startled him. Off to the right he heard it, and his ears, expert in such matters, could not be mistaken. Again he heard the sound, and again. Somewhere, off in the blackness, someone had fired a gun three times.

Rainsford sprang up and moved quickly to the rail, mystified. He strained his eyes in the direction from which the reports had come, but it was like trying to see through a blanket. He leaped upon the rail and balanced himself there, to get greater elevation; his pipe, striking a rope, was knocked from his mouth. He lunged for it; a short, hoarse cry came from his lips as he realized he had reached too far and had lost his balance. The cry was pinched off short as the blood-warm waters of the Caribbean Sea closed over his head.

He struggled up to the surface and tried to cry out, but the wash from the speeding yacht slapped him in the face and the salt water in his open mouth made him gag and strangle. Desperately he struck out with strong strokes after the receding lights of the yacht, but he stopped before he had swum fifty feet. A certain cool-headedness had come to him; it was not the first time he had been in a tight place. There was a chance that his cries could be heard by someone aboard the yacht, but that chance was slender and grew more slender as the yacht raced on. He wrestled himself out of his clothes and shouted with all his power. The lights of the yacht became faint and ever-vanishing fireflies; then they were blotted out entirely by the night.

Rainsford remembered the shots. They had come from the right, and doggedly he swam in that direction, swimming with slow, deliberate strokes, conserving his strength. For a seemingly endless time he fought the sea. He began to count his strokes; he could do possibly a hundred more and then—

Rainsford heard a sound. It came out of the darkness, a high screaming sound, the sound of an animal in an extremity of anguish and terror.

He did not recognize the animal that made the sound; he did not try to; with fresh vitality he swam toward the sound. He heard it again; then it was cut short by another noise, crisp, staccato.

"Pistol shot," muttered Rainsford, swimming on.

Ten minutes of determined effort brought another sound to his ears—the most welcome he had ever heard—the muttering and growling of the sea breaking on a rocky shore. He was almost on the rocks before he saw them; on a night less calm he would have been shattered against them. With his remaining strength he dragged himself from the swirling waters. Jagged crags appeared to jut up into the opaqueness; he forced himself upward, hand over hand. Gasping, his hands raw, he reached a flat place at the top. Dense jungle came down to the very edge of the cliffs. What perils that tangle of trees and underbrush might hold for him did not concern Rainsford just then. All he knew was that he was safe from his enemy, the sea, and that utter weariness was on him. He flung himself down at the jungle edge and tumbled headlong into the deepest sleep of his life.

When he opened his eyes he knew from the position of the sun that it was late in the afternoon. Sleep had given him new vigor; a sharp hunger was picking at him. He looked about him, almost cheerfully.

"Where there are pistol shots, there are men. Where there are men, there is food," he thought. But what kind of men, he wondered, in so forbidding a place? An unbroken front of snarled and ragged jungle fringed the shore.

He saw no sign of a trail through the closely knit web of weeds and trees; it was easier to go along the shore, and Rainsford floundered along by the water. Not far from where he landed, he stopped.

Some wounded thing—by the evidence, a large animal—had thrashed about in the underbrush; the jungle weeds were crushed down and the moss was lacerated; one patch of weeds was stained crimson. A small, glittering object not far away caught Rainsford's eye and he picked it up. It was an empty cartridge.

"A twenty-two," he remarked. "That's odd. It must have been a fairly large animal too. The hunter had his nerve with him to tackle it with a light gun. It's clear that the brute put up a fight. I suppose the first three shots I heard was when the hunter flushed his quarry and wounded it. The last shot was when he trailed it here and finished it."

He examined the ground closely and found what he had hoped to find—the print of hunting boots. They pointed along the cliff in the direction he had been going. Eagerly he hurried along, now slipping on a rotten log or a loose stone, but making headway; night was beginning to settle down on the island.

Bleak darkness was blacking out the sea and jungle when Rainsford sighted the lights. He came upon them as he turned a crook in the coast line; and his first thought was that he had come upon a village, for there were many lights. But as he forged along he saw to his great astonishment that all the lights were in one enormous building—a lofty structure with pointed towers plunging upward into the gloom. His eyes made out the shadowy outlines of a palatial chateau; it was set on a high bluff, and on three sides of it cliffs dived down to where the sea licked greedy lips in the shadows.

"Mirage," thought Rainsford. But it was no mirage, he found, when he opened the tall spiked iron gate. The stone steps were real enough; the massive door with a leering gargoyle for a knocker was real enough; yet above it all hung an air of unreality.

He lifted the knocker, and it creaked up stiffly, as if it had never before been used. He let it fall, and it startled him with its booming loudness. He thought he heard steps within; the door remained closed. Again Rainsford lifted the heavy knocker, and let it fall. The door opened then—opened as suddenly as if it were on a spring—and Rainsford stood blinking in the river of glaring gold light that poured out. The first thing Rainsford's eyes discerned was the largest man Rainsford had ever seen—a gigantic creature, solidly made and black bearded to the waist. In his hand the man held a long-barreled revolver, and he was pointing it straight at Rainsford's heart.

Out of the snarl of beard two small eyes regarded Rainsford.

"Don't be alarmed," said Rainsford, with a smile which he hoped was disarming. "I'm no robber. I fell off a yacht. My name is Sanger Rainsford of New York City."

The menacing look in the eyes did not change. The revolver pointed as rigidly as if the giant were a statue. He gave no sign that he understood Rainsford's words, or that he had even heard them. He was dressed in uniform—a black uniform trimmed with gray astrakhan.

"I'm Sanger Rainsford of New York," Rainsford began again. "I fell off a yacht. I am hungry."

The man's only answer was to raise with his thumb the hammer of his revolver. Then Rainsford saw the man's free hand go to his forehead in a military salute, and he saw him click his heels together and stand at attention. Another man was coming down the broad marble steps, an erect, slender man in evening clothes. He advanced to Rainsford and held out his hand.

In a cultivated voice marked by a slight accent that gave it added precision and deliberateness, he said, "It is a very great pleasure and honor to welcome Mr. Sanger Rainsford, the celebrated hunter, to my home."

Automatically Rainsford shook the man's hand.

"I've read your book about hunting snow leopards in Tibet, you see," explained the man. "I am General Zaroff."

Rainsford's first impression was that the man was singularly handsome; his second was that there was an original, almost bizarre quality about the general's face. He was a tall man past middle age, for his hair was a vivid white; but his thick eyebrows and pointed military mustache were as black as the night from which Rainsford had come. His eyes, too, were black and very bright. He had high cheekbones, a sharp-cut nose, a spare, dark face—the face of a man used to giving orders, the face of an aristocrat. Turning to the giant in uniform, the general made a sign. The giant put away his pistol, saluted, withdrew.

"Ivan is an incredibly strong fellow," remarked the general, "but he has the misfortune to be deaf and dumb. A simple fellow, but, I'm afraid, like all his race, a bit of a savage."

"Is he Russian?"

"He is a Cossack," said the general, and his smile showed red lips and pointed teeth. "So am I."

"Come," he said, "we shouldn't be chatting here. We can talk later. Now you want clothes, food, rest. You shall have them. This is a most-restful spot."

Ivan had reappeared, and the general spoke to him with lips that moved but gave forth no sound.

"Follow Ivan, if you please, Mr. Rainsford," said the general. "I was about to have my dinner when you came. I'll wait for you. You'll find that my clothes will fit you, I think."

It was to a huge, beam-ceilinged bedroom with a canopied bed big enough for six men that Rainsford followed the silent giant. Ivan laid out an evening suit, and Rainsford, as he put it on, noticed that it came from a London tailor who ordinarily cut and sewed for none below the rank of duke.

The dining room to which Ivan conducted him was in many ways remarkable. There was a medieval magnificence about it; it suggested a baronial hall of feudal times with its oaken panels, its high ceiling, its vast refectory tables where two-score men could sit down to eat. About the hall were mounted heads of many animals—lions, tigers, elephants, moose, bears; larger or more perfect specimens Rainsford had never seen. At the great table the general was sitting, alone.

"You'll have a cocktail, Mr. Rainsford," he suggested. The cocktail was surpassingly good; and, Rainsford noted, the table appointments were of the finest—the linen, the crystal, the silver, the china.

They were eating *borscht,* the rich, red soup with whipped cream so dear to Russian palates. Half apologetically General Zaroff said, "We do our best to preserve the amenities of civilization here. Please forgive any lapses. We are well off the beaten track, you know. Do you think the champagne has suffered from its long ocean trip?"

"Not in the least," declared Rainsford. He was finding the general a most thoughtful and affable host, a true cosmopolite. But there was one small trait of the general's that made Rainsford uncomfortable. Whenever he looked up from his plate he found the general studying him, appraising him narrowly.

"Perhaps," said General Zaroff, "you were surprised that I recognized your name. You see, I read all books on hunting published in English, French, and Russian. I have but one passion in my life, Mr. Rainsford, and it is the hunt."

"You have some wonderful heads here," said Rainsford as he ate a particularly well-cooked filet mignon. "That Cape buffalo is the largest I ever saw."

"Oh, that fellow. Yes, he was a monster."

"Did he charge you?"

"Hurled me against a tree," said the general. "Fractured my skull. But I got the brute."

"I've always thought," said Rainsford, "that the Cape buffalo is the most dangerous of all big game."

For a moment the general did not reply; he was smiling his curious red-lipped smile. Then he said slowly, "No. You are wrong, sir. The Cape buffalo is not the most dangerous big game." He sipped his wine. "Here in my preserve on this island," he said in the same slow tone, "I hunt more dangerous game."

Rainsford expressed his surprise. "Is there big game on this island?"

The general nodded. "The biggest."

"Really?"

"Oh, it isn't here naturally, of course. I have to stock the island."

"What have you imported, general?" Rainsford asked. "Tigers?"

The general smiled. "No," he said. "Hunting tigers ceased to interest me some years ago. I exhausted their possibilities, you see. No thrill left in tigers, no real danger. I live for danger, Mr. Rainsford."

The general took from his pocket a gold cigarette case and offered his guest a long black cigarette with a silver tip; it was perfumed and gave off a smell like incense.

"We will have some capital hunting, you and I," said the general. "I shall be most glad to have your society."

"But what game—" began Rainsford.

"I'll tell you," said the general. "You will be amused, I know. I think I may say, in all modesty, that I have done a rare thing. I have invented a new sensation. May I pour you another glass of port?"

"Thank you, general."

The general filled both glasses, and said, "God makes some men poets. Some He makes kings, some beggars. Me He made a hunter. My hand was made for the trigger, my father said. He was a very rich man with a quarter of a million acres in the Crimea, and he was an ardent sportsman. When I was only five years old he gave me a little gun, specially made in Moscow for me, to shoot sparrows with. When I shot some of his prize turkeys with it, he did not punish me; he complimented me on my marksmanship. I killed my first bear in the Caucasus when I was ten. My whole life has been one prolonged hunt. I went into the army—it was expected of noblemen's sons—and for a time commanded a division of Cossack cavalry, but my real interest was always the hunt. I have hunted every kind of game in every land. It would be impossible for me to tell you how many animals I have killed."

The general puffed at his cigarette.

"After the debacle in Russia I left the country, for it was imprudent for an officer of the Czar to stay there. Many noble Russians lost everything. I, luckily, had invested heavily in American securities, so I shall never have to open a tea room in Monte Carlo or drive a taxi in Paris. Naturally, I continued to hunt—grizzlies in your Rockies, crocodiles in the Ganges, rhinoceroses in East Africa. It was in Africa that the Cape buffalo hit me and laid me up for six months. As soon as I recovered I started for the Amazon to hunt jaguars, for I had heard they were unusually cunning. They weren't." The Cossack sighed. "They were no match at all for a hunter with his wits about him, and a high-powered rifle. I was bitterly disappointed. I was lying in my tent with a splitting headache one night when a terrible thought pushed its way into my mind. Hunting was beginning to bore me! And hunting, remember, had been my life. I have heard that in America businessmen often go to pieces when they give up the business that has been their life."

"Yes, that's so," said Rainsford.

The general smiled. "I had no wish to go to pieces," he said. "I must do something. Now, mine is an analytical mind, Mr. Rainsford. Doubtless that is why I enjoy the problems of the chase."

"No doubt, General Zaroff."

"So," continued the general, "I asked myself why the hunt no longer fascinated me. You are much younger than I am, Mr. Rainsford, and have not hunted as much, but you perhaps can guess the answer."

"What was it?"

"Simply this: hunting had ceased to be what you call 'a sporting proposition.' It had become too easy. I always got my quarry. Always. There is no greater bore than perfection."

The general lit a fresh cigarette.

"No animal had a chance with me any more. That is no boast; it is a mathematical certainty. The animal had nothing but his legs and his instinct. Instinct is no match for reason. When I thought of this it was a tragic moment for me, I can tell you."

Rainsford leaned across the table, absorbed in what his host was saying.

"It came to me as an inspiration what I must do," the general went on.

"And that was?"

The general smiled the quiet smile of one who has faced an obstacle and surmounted it with success. "I had to invent a new animal to hunt," he said.

"A new animal? You're joking."

"Not at all," said the general. "I never joke about hunting. I needed a new animal. I found one. So I bought this island built this house, and here I do my hunting. The island is perfect for my purposes— there are jungles with a maze of trails in them, hills, swamps—"

"But the animal, General Zaroff?"

"Oh," said the general, "it supplies me with the most exciting hunting in the world. No other hunting compares with it for an instant. Every day I hunt, and I never grow bored now, for I have a quarry with which I can match my wits."

Rainsford's bewilderment showed in his face.

"I wanted the ideal animal to hunt," explained the general. "So I said, 'What are the attributes of an ideal quarry?' And the answer was, of course, 'It must have courage, cunning, and, above all, it must be able to reason.'"

"But no animal can reason," objected Rainsford.

"My dear fellow," said the general, "there is one that can."

"But you can't mean—" gasped Rainsford.

"And why not?"

"I can't believe you are serious, General Zaroff. This is a grisly joke."

"Why should I not be serious? I am speaking of hunting."

"Hunting? Great God, General Zaroff, what you speak of is murder."

The general laughed with entire good nature. He regarded Rainsford quizzically. "I refuse to believe that so modern and civilized a young man as you seem to be harbors romantic ideas about the value of human life. Surely your experiences in the war—" He stopped.

"Did not make me condone cold-blooded murder," finished Rainsford stiffly.

Laughter shook the general. "How extraordinarily droll you are!" he said. "One does not expect nowadays to find a young man of the educated class, even in America, with such a naïve, and, if I may say so, mid-Victorian point of view. It's like finding a snuffbox in a limousine. Ah, well, doubtless you had Puritan ancestors. So many Americans appear to have had. I'll wager you'll forget your notions when you go hunting with me. You've a genuine new thrill in store for you, Mr. Rainsford."

"Thank you, I'm a hunter, not a murderer."

"Dear me," said the general, quite unruffled, "again that unpleasant word. But I think I can show you that your scruples are quite ill founded."

"Yes?"

"Life is for the strong, to be lived by the strong, and, if needs be, taken by the strong. The weak of the world were put here to give the strong pleasure. I am strong. Why should I not use my gift? If I wish to hunt, why should I not? I hunt the scum of the earth: sailors from tramp ships—lascars, blacks, Chinese, whites, mongrels—a thoroughbred horse or hound is worth more than a score of them."

"But they are men," said Rainsford hotly.

"Precisely," said the general. "That is why I use them. It gives me pleasure. They can reason, after a fashion. So they are dangerous."

"But where do you get them?"

The general's left eyelid fluttered down in a wink. "This island is called Ship-Trap," he answered. "Sometimes an angry god of the high seas sends them to me. Sometimes, when Providence is not so kind, I help Providence a bit. Come to the window with me."

Rainsford went to the window and looked out toward the sea.

"Watch! Out there!" exclaimed the general, pointing into the night. Rainsford's eyes saw only blackness, and then, as the general pressed a button, far out to sea Rainsford saw the flash of lights.

The general chuckled. "They indicate a channel," he said, "where there's none; giant rocks with razor edges crouch like a sea monster with wide-open jaws. They can crush a ship as easily as I crush this nut." He dropped a walnut on the hardwood floor and brought his heel grinding down on it. "Oh, yes," he said, casually, as if in answer to a question, "I have electricity. We try to be civilized here."

"Civilized? And you shoot down men?"

A trace of anger was in the general's black eyes, but it was there for but a second; and he said, in his most pleasant manner, "Dear me, what a righteous young man you are! I assure you I do not do the thing you suggest. That would be barbarous. I treat these visitors with every consideration. They get plenty of good food and exercise. They get into splendid physical condition. You shall see for yourself tomorrow."

"What do you mean?"

"We'll visit my training school," smiled the general. "It's in the cellar. I have about a dozen pupils down there now. They're from the Spanish bark *San Lucar* that had the bad luck to go on the rocks out there. A very inferior lot, I regret to say. Poor specimens and more accustomed to the deck than to the jungle."

He raised his hand, and Ivan, who served as waiter, brought thick Turkish coffee. Rainsford, with an effort, held his tongue in check.

"It's a game, you see," pursued the general blandly. "I suggest to one of them that we go hunting. I give him a supply of food and an excellent hunting knife. I give him three hours' start. I am to follow, armed only with a pistol of the smallest caliber and range. If my quarry eludes me for three whole days, he wins the game. If I find him"—the general smiled—"he loses."

"Suppose he refuses to be hunted?"

"Oh," said the general, "I give him his option, of course. He need not play that game if he doesn't wish to. If he does not wish to hunt, I turn him over to Ivan. Ivan once had the honor of serving as official knouter to the Great White Czar, and he has his own ideas of sport. Invariably, Mr. Rainsford, invariably they choose the hunt."

"And if they win?"

The smile on the general's face widened. "To date I have not lost," he said.

Then he added, hastily: "I don't wish you to think me a braggart, Mr. Rainsford. Many of them afford only the most elementary sort of problem. Occasionally I strike a tartar. One almost did win. I eventually had to use the dogs."

"The dogs?"

"This way, please. I'll show you."

The general steered Rainsford to a window. The lights from the windows sent a flickering illumination that made grotesque patterns on the courtyard below, and Rainsford could see moving about there a dozen or so huge black shapes; as they turned toward him, their eyes glittered greenly.

"A rather good lot, I think," observed the general. "They are let out at seven every night. If anyone should try to get into my house— or out of it—something extremely regrettable would occur to him." He hummed a snatch of song from the *Folies Bergère*.

"And now," said the general, "I want to show you my new collection of heads. Will you come with me to the library?"

"I hope," said Rainsford, "that you will excuse me tonight, General Zaroff. I'm really not feeling well."

"Ah, indeed?" the general inquired solicitously. "Well, I suppose that's only natural, after your long swim. You need a good, restful night's sleep. Tomorrow you'll feel like a new man, I'll wager. Then we'll hunt, eh? I've one rather promising prospect—"

Rainsford was hurrying from the room.

"Sorry you can't go with me tonight," called the general. "I expect rather fair sport—a big, strong, black. He looks resourceful— Well, good night, Mr. Rainsford; I hope you have a good night's rest."

The bed was good, and the pajamas of the softest silk, and he was tired in every fiber of his being, but nevertheless Rainsford could not quiet his brain with the opiate of sleep. He lay, eyes wide open. Once he thought he heard stealthy steps in the corridor outside his room. He sought to throw open the door; it would not open. He went to the window and looked out. His room was high up in one of the towers. The lights of the chateau were out now, and it was dark and silent; but there was a fragment of sallow moon, and by its wan light he could see, dimly, the courtyard. There, weaving in and out in the pattern of shadow, were black, noiseless forms; the hounds heard him at the window and looked up, expectantly, with their green eyes. Rainsford went back to the bed and lay down. By many methods he tried to put himself to sleep. He had achieved a doze when, just as morning began to come, he heard, far off in the jungle, the faint report of a pistol.

* * *

General Zaroff did not appear until luncheon. He was dressed fault-
lessly in the tweeds of a country squire. He was solicitous about the
state of Rainsford's health.

"As for me," sighed the general, "I do not feel so well. I am worried,
Mr. Rainsford. Last night I detected traces of my old complaint."

To Rainsford's questioning glance the general said, "*Ennui.*
Boredom."

Then, taking a second helping of *crêpes Suzette,* the general
explained: "The hunting was not good last night. The fellow lost his
head. He made a straight trail that offered no problems at all. That's
the trouble with these sailors; they have dull brains to begin with,
and they do not know how to get about in the woods. They do
excessively stupid and obvious things. It's most annoying. Will you
have another glass of *Chablis,* Mr. Rainsford?"

"General," said Rainsford firmly, "I wish to leave this island at
once."

The general raised his thickets of eyebrows; he seemed hurt. "But,
my dear fellow," the general protested, "you've only just come.
You've had no hunting—"

"I wish to go today," said Rainsford. He saw the dead black eyes
of the general on him, studying him. General Zaroff's face suddenly
brightened.

He filled Rainsford's glass with venerable *Chablis* from a dusty
bottle.

"Tonight," said the general, "we will hunt—you and I."

Rainsford shook his head. "No, general," he said. "I will not hunt."

The general shrugged his shoulders and delicately ate a hothouse
grape. "As you wish, my friend," he said. "The choice rests entirely
with you. But may I not venture to suggest that you will find my
idea of sport more diverting than Ivan's?"

He nodded toward the corner to where the giant stood, scowling,
his thick arms crossed on his hogshead of chest.

"You don't mean—" cried Rainsford.

"My dear fellow," said the general, "have I not told you I always
mean what I say about hunting? This is really an inspiration. I drink
to a foeman worthy of my steel—at last."

The general raised his glass, but Rainsford sat staring at him.

"You'll find this game worth playing," the general said enthusi-
astically. "Your brain against mine. Your woodcraft against mine.

Your strength and stamina against mine. Outdoor chess! And the stake is not without value, eh?"

"And if I win—" began Rainsford huskily.

"I'll cheerfully acknowledge myself defeated if I do not find you by midnight of the third day," said General Zaroff. "My sloop will place you on the mainland near a town."

The general read what Rainsford was thinking.

"Oh, you can trust me," said the Cossack. "I will give you my word as a gentleman and a sportsman. Of course you, in turn, must agree to say nothing of your visit here."

"I'll agree to nothing of the kind," said Rainsford.

"Oh," said the general, "in that case—But why discuss that now? Three days hence we can discuss it over a bottle of *Veuve Cliquot,* unless—"

The general sipped his wine.

Then a businesslike air animated him. "Ivan," he said to Rainsford, "will supply you with hunting clothes, food, a knife. I suggest you wear moccasins; they leave a poorer trail. I suggest, too, that you avoid the big swamp in the southeast corner of the island. We call it Death Swamp. There's quicksand there. One foolish fellow tried it. The deplorable part of it was that Lazarus followed him. You can imagine my feelings, Mr. Rainsford. I loved Lazarus; he was the finest hound in my pack. Well, I must beg you to excuse me now. I always take a siesta after lunch. You'll hardly have time for a nap, I fear. You'll want to start, no doubt. I shall not follow till dusk. Hunting at night is so much more exciting than by day, don't you think? *Au revoir,* Mr. Rainsford, *au revoir.*"

General Zaroff, with a deep, courtly bow, strolled from the room.

From another door came Ivan. Under one arm he carried khaki hunting clothes, a haversack of food, a leather sheath containing a long-bladed hunting knife; his right hand rested on a cocked revolver thrust in the crimson sash about his waist. . . .

Rainsford had fought his way through the bush for two hours. "I must keep my nerve. I must keep my nerve," he said through tight teeth.

He had not been entirely clearheaded when the chateau gates snapped shut behind him. His whole idea at first was to put distance between himself and General Zaroff; and, to this end, he had plunged along, spurred on by the sharp rowels of something very like panic. Now he had got a grip on himself, had stopped, and was taking stock of himself and the situation.

He saw that straight flight was futile; inevitably it would bring him face to face with the sea. He was in a picture with a frame of water, and his operations, clearly, must take place within that frame.

"I'll give him a trail to follow," muttered Rainsford, and he struck off from the rude path he had been following into the trackless wilderness. He executed a series of intricate loops; he doubled on his trail again and again, recalling all the lore of the fox hunt, and all the dodges of the fox. Night found him leg-weary, with hands and face lashed by the branches, on a thickly wooded ridge. He knew it would be insane to blunder on through the dark, even if he had the strength. His need for rest was imperative and he thought, "I have played the fox, now I must play the cat of the fable." A big tree with a thick trunk and outspread branches was near by, and, taking care to leave not the slightest mark, he climbed up into the crotch, and, stretching out on one of the broad limbs, after a fashion, rested. Rest brought him new confidence and almost a feeling of security. Even so zealous a hunter as General Zaroff could not trace him there, he told himself; only the devil himself could follow that complicated trail through the jungle after dark. But perhaps the general was a devil—

An apprehensive night crawled slowly by like a wounded snake and sleep did not visit Rainsford, although the silence of a dead world was on the jungle. Toward morning when a dingy gray was varnishing the sky, the cry of some startled bird focused Rainsford's attention in that direction. Something was coming through the bush, coming slowly, carefully, coming by the same winding way Rainsford had come. He flattened himself down on the limb and, through a screen of leaves almost as thick as tapestry, he watched. The thing that was approaching was a man.

It was General Zaroff. He made his way along with his eyes fixed in utmost concentration on the ground before him. He paused, almost beneath the tree, dropped to his knees and studied the ground. Rainsford's impulse was to hurl himself down like a panther, but he saw that the general's right hand held something metallic—a small automatic pistol.

The hunter shook his head several times, as if he were puzzled. Then he straightened up and took from his case one of his black cigarettes; its pungent incense-like smoke floated up to Rainsford's nostrils. Rainsford held his breath. The general's eyes had left the ground and were traveling inch by inch up the tree. Rainsford froze there, every muscle tensed for a spring. But the sharp eyes of the hunter stopped before they reached the limb where Rainsford lay; a smile spread over his brown face. Very deliberately he blew a smoke ring into the air; then he turned his back on the tree and walked carelessly away, back along the trail he had come. The swish of the underbrush against his hunting boots grew fainter and fainter.

The pent-up air burst hotly from Rainsford's lungs. His first thought made him feel sick and numb. The general could follow a trail through the woods at night; he could follow an extremely difficult trail; he must have uncanny powers; only by the merest chance had the Cossack failed to see his quarry.

Rainsford's second thought was even more terrible. It sent a shudder of cold horror through his whole being. Why had the general smiled? Why had he turned back?

Rainsford did not want to believe what his reason told him was true, but the truth was as evident as the sun that had by now pushed through the morning mists. The general was playing with him! The general was saving him for another day's sport! The Cossack was the cat; he was the mouse. Then it was that Rainsford knew the full meaning of terror.

"I will not lose my nerve. I will not."

He slid down from the tree, and struck off again into the woods. His face was set and he forced the machinery of his mind to function. Three hundred yards from his hiding place he stopped where a huge dead tree leaned precariously on a smaller, living one. Throwing off his sack of food, Rainsford took his knife from its sheath and began to work with all his energy.

The job was finished at last, and he threw himself down behind a fallen log a hundred feet away. He did not have to wait long. The cat was coming again to play with the mouse.

Following the trail with the sureness of a bloodhound came General Zaroff. Nothing escaped those searching black eyes, no crushed blade of grass, no bent twig, no mark, no matter how faint, in the moss. So intent was the Cossack on his stalking that he was upon the thing Rainsford had made before he saw it. His foot touched the protruding bough that was the trigger. Even as he touched it, the general sensed his danger and leaped back with the agility of an ape. But he was not quite quick enough; the dead tree, delicately adjusted to rest on the cut living one, crashed down and struck the general a glancing blow on the shoulder as it fell; but for his alertness, he must have been smashed beneath it. He staggered, but he did not fall; nor did he drop his revolver. He stood there, rubbing his injured shoulder, and Rainsford, with fear again gripping his heart, heard the general's mocking laugh ring through the jungle.

"Rainsford," called the general, "if you are within sound of my voice, as I suppose you are, let me congratulate you. Not many men know how to make a Malay man-catcher. Luckily for me I, too, have hunted in Malacca. You are proving interesting, Mr. Rainsford. I am going now to have my wound dressed; it's only a slight one. But I shall be back. I shall be back."

When the general, nursing his bruised shoulder, had gone, Rainsford took up his flight again. It was flight now, a desperate, hopeless flight, that carried him on for some hours. Dusk came, then darkness, and still he pressed on. The ground grew softer under his moccasins; the vegetation grew ranker, denser; insects bit him savagely. Then, as he stepped forward, his foot sank into the ooze. He tried to wrench it back, but the muck sucked viciously at his foot as if it were a giant leech. With a violent effort, he tore his feet loose. He knew where he was now. Death Swamp and its quicksand.

His hands were tight closed as if his nerve were something tangible that someone in the darkness was trying to tear from his grip. The softness of the earth had given him an idea. He stepped back from the quicksand a dozen feet or so and, like some huge prehistoric beaver, he began to dig.

Rainsford had dug himself in in France when a second's delay meant death. That had been a placid pastime compared to his digging now. The pit grew deeper; when it was above his shoulders, he climbed out and from some hard saplings cut stakes and sharpened them to a fine point. These stakes he planted in the bottom of the pit with the points sticking up. With flying fingers he wove a rough carpet of weeds and branches and with it he covered the mouth of the pit. Then, wet with sweat and aching with tiredness, he crouched behind the stump of a lightning-charred tree.

He knew his pursuer was coming; he heard the padding sound of feet on the soft earth, and the night breeze brought him the perfume of the general's cigarette. It seemed to Rainsford that the general was coming with unusual swiftness; he was not feeling his way along, foot by foot. Rainsford, crouching there, could not see the general, nor could he see the pit. He lived a year in a minute. Then he felt an impulse to cry aloud with joy, for he heard the sharp crackle of the breaking branches as the cover of the pit gave way; he heard the sharp scream of pain as the pointed stakes found their mark. He leaped up from his place of concealment. Then he cowered back. Three feet from the pit a man was standing, with an electric torch in his hand.

"You've done well, Rainsford," the voice of the general called. "Your Burmese tiger pit has claimed one of my best dogs. Again you score. I think, Mr. Rainsford, I'll see what you can do against my whole pack. I'm going home for a rest now. Thank you for a most amusing evening."

At daybreak Rainsford, lying near the swamp, was awakened by a sound that made him know that he had new things to learn about fear. It was a distant sound, faint and wavering, but he knew it. It was the baying of a pack of hounds.

Rainsford knew he could do one of two things. He could stay where he was and wait. That was suicide. He could flee. That was postponing the inevitable. For a moment he stood there, thinking. An idea that held a wild chance came to him, and, tightening his belt, he headed away from the swamp.

The baying of the hounds drew nearer, then still nearer, nearer, ever nearer. On a ridge Rainsford climbed a tree. Down a water-course, not a quarter of a mile away, he could see the bush moving. Straining his eyes, he saw the lean figure of General Zaroff; just ahead of him Rainsford made out another figure whose wide shoulders surged through the tall jungle weeds; it was the giant Ivan, and he seemed pulled forward by some unseen force; Rainsford knew that Ivan must be holding the pack in leash.

They would be on him any minute now. His mind worked frantically. He thought of a native trick he had learned in Uganda. He slid down the tree. He caught hold of a springy young sapling and to it he fastened his hunting knife, with the blade pointing down the trail; with a bit of wild grapevine he tied back the sapling. Then he ran for his life. The hounds raised their voices as they hit the fresh scent. Rainsford knew now how an animal at bay feels.

He had to stop to get his breath. The baying of the hounds stopped abruptly, and Rainsford's heart stopped too. They must have reached the knife.

He shinned excitedly up a tree and looked back. His pursuers had stopped. But the hope that was in Rainsford's brain when he climbed died, for he saw in the shallow valley that General Zaroff was still on his feet. But Ivan was not. The knife, driven by the recoil of the springing tree, had not wholly failed.

Rainsford had hardly tumbled to the ground when the pack took up the cry again.

"Nerve, nerve, nerve!" he panted, as he dashed along. A blue gap showed between the trees dead ahead. Ever nearer drew the hounds. Rainsford forced himself on toward that gap. He reached it. It was the shore of the sea. Across a cove he could see the gloomy gray stone of the chateau. Twenty feet below him the sea rumbled and hissed. Rainsford hesitated. He heard the hounds. Then he leaped far out into the sea. . . .

When the general and his pack reached the place by the sea, the Cossack stopped. For some minutes he stood regarding the blue-green expanse of water. He shrugged his shoulders. Then he sat down, took a drink of brandy from a silver flask, lit a cigarette, and hummed a bit from *Madame Butterfly*.

General Zaroff had an exceedingly good dinner in his great paneled dining hall that evening. With it he had a bottle of *Pol Roger* and half a bottle of *Chambertin*. Two slight annoyances kept him from perfect enjoyment. One was the thought that it would be difficult to replace Ivan; the other was that his quarry had escaped him; of course, the American hadn't played the game—so thought the general as he tasted his after-dinner liqueur. In his library he read, to soothe himself, from the works of Marcus Aurelius. At ten he went up to his bedroom. He was deliciously tired, he said to himself, as he locked himself in. There was a little moonlight, so, before turning on his light, he went to the window and looked down at the courtyard. He could see the great hounds, and he called, "Better luck another time," to them. Then he switched on the light.

A man, who had been hiding in the curtains of the bed, was standing there.

"Rainsford!" screamed the general. "How in God's name did you get here?"

"Swam," said Rainsford. "I found it quicker than walking through the jungle."

The general sucked in his breath and smiled. "I congratulate you," he said. "You have won the game."

Rainsford did not smile. "I am still a beast at bay," he said, in a low, hoarse voice. "Get ready, General Zaroff."

The general made one of his deepest bows. "I see," he said. "Splendid! One of us is to furnish a repast for the hounds. The other will sleep in this very excellent bed. On guard, Rainsford." . . .

He had never slept in a better bed, Rainsford decided.

TO BUILD A FIRE

Jack London

DAY HAD BROKEN cold and gray, exceedingly cold and gray, when the man turned aside from the main Yukon trail and climbed the high earth-bank, where a dim and little-travelled trail led eastward through the fat spruce timberland. It was a steep bank, and he paused for breath at the top, excusing the act to himself by looking at his watch. It was nine o'clock. There was no sun nor hint of sun, though there was not a cloud in the sky. It was a clear day, and yet there seemed an intangible pall over the face of things, a subtle gloom that made the day dark, and that was due to the absence of sun. This fact did not worry the man. He was used to the lack of sun. It had been days since he had seen the sun, and he knew that a few more days must pass before that cheerful orb, due south, would just peep above the sky-line and dip immediately from view.

The man flung a look back along the way he had come. The Yukon lay a mile wide and hidden under three feet of ice. On top of this ice were as many feet of snow. It was all pure white, rolling in gentle undulations where the ice-jams of the freeze-up had formed. North and south, as far as his eye could see, it was unbroken white, save for a dark hair-line that curved and twisted from around the spruce-covered island to the south, and that curved and twisted away into the north, where it disappeared behind another spruce-covered island. This dark hair-line was the trail—the main trail—that led south five hundred miles to the Chilcoot Pass, Dyea, and salt water; and that led north seventy miles to Dawson, and still on to the north a thousand miles to Nulato, and finally to St. Michael on Bering Sea, a thousand miles and half a thousand more.

But all this—the mysterious, far-reaching hair-line trail, the absence of sun from the sky, the tremendous cold, and the strangeness and weirdness of it all—made no impression on the man. It was not because he was long used to it. He was a newcomer in the land, a *chechaquo,* and this was his first winter. The trouble with him was that he was without imagination. He was quick and alert in the things of life, but only in the things, and not in the significances. Fifty degrees below zero meant eighty-odd degrees of frost. Such fact impressed him as being cold and uncomfortable, and that was all. It did not lead him to meditate upon his frailty as a creature of temperature, and upon man's frailty in general, able only to live within certain narrow limits of heat and cold; and from there on it did not lead him to the conjectural field of immortality and man's place in the universe. Fifty degrees below zero stood for a bite of frost that hurt and that must be guarded against by the use of mittens, ear-flaps, warm moccasins, and thick socks. Fifty degrees below zero was to him just precisely fifty degrees below zero. That there should be anything more to it than that was a thought that never entered his head.

As he turned to go on, he spat speculatively. There was a sharp, explosive crackle that startled him. He spat again. And again, in the air, before it could fall to the snow, the spittle crackled. He knew that at fifty below spittle crackled on the snow, but this spittle had crackled in the air. Undoubtedly it was colder than fifty below—how much colder he did not know. But the temperature did not matter. He was bound for the old claim on the left fork of Henderson Creek, where the boys were already. They had come over across the divide from the Indian Creek country, while he had come the roundabout way to take a look at the possibilities of getting out logs in the spring from the islands in the Yukon. He would be in to camp by six o'clock; a bit after dark, it was true, but the boys would be there, a fire would be going, and a hot supper would be ready. As for lunch, he pressed his hand against the protruding bundle under his jacket. It was also under his shirt, wrapped up in a handkerchief and lying against the naked skin. It was the only way to keep the biscuits from freezing. He smiled agreeably to himself as he thought of those biscuits, each cut open and sopped in bacon grease, and each enclosing a generous slice of fried bacon.

He plunged in among the big spruce trees. The trail was faint. A foot of snow had fallen since the last sled had passed over, and he was glad he was without a sled, travelling light. In fact, he carried nothing but the lunch wrapped in the handkerchief. He was surprised, however, at the cold. It certainly was cold, he concluded, as he rubbed his numb nose and cheek-bones with his mittened hand. He was a warm-whiskered man, but the hair on his face did not protect the high cheek-bones and the eager nose that thrust itself aggressively into the frosty air.

At the man's heels trotted a dog, a big native husky, the proper wolf-dog, gray-coated and without any visible or temperamental difference from its brother, the wild wolf. The animal was depressed by the tremendous cold. It knew that it was no time for travelling. Its instinct told it a truer tale than was told to the man by the man's judgment. In reality, it was not merely colder than fifty below zero; it was colder than sixty below, than seventy below. It was seventy-five below zero. Since the freezing-point is thirty-two above zero, it meant that one hundred and seven degrees of frost obtained. The dog did not know anything about thermometers. Possibly in its brain there was no sharp consciousness of a condition of very cold such as was in the man's brain. But the brute had its instinct. It experienced a vague but menacing apprehension that subdued it and made it slink along at the man's heels, and that made it question eagerly every unwonted movement of the man as if expecting him to go into camp or to seek shelter somewhere and build a fire. The dog had learned fire, and it wanted fire, or else to burrow under the snow and cuddle its warmth away from the air.

The frozen moisture of its breathing had settled on its fur in a fine powder of frost, and especially were its jowls, muzzle, and eyelashes whitened by its crystalled breath. The man's red beard and mustache were likewise frosted, but more solidly, the deposit taking the form of ice and increasing with every warm, moist breath he exhaled. Also, the man was chewing tobacco, and the muzzle of ice held his lips so rigidly that he was unable to clear his chin when he expelled the juice. The result was that a crystal beard of the color and solidity of amber was increasing its length on his chin. If he fell down it would shatter itself, like glass, into brittle fragments. But he did not mind the appendage. It was the penalty all tobacco-chewers paid in that country, and he had been out before in two cold snaps. They had not been so cold as this, he knew, but by the spirit thermometer at Sixty Mile he knew they had been registered at fifty below and at fifty-five.

He held on through the level stretch of woods for several miles, crossed a wide flat of niggerheads, and dropped down a bank to the frozen bed of a small stream. This was Henderson Creek, and he knew he was ten miles from the forks. He looked at his watch. It was ten o'clock. He was making four miles an hour, and he calculated that he would arrive at the forks at half-past twelve. He decided to celebrate that event by eating his lunch there.

The dog dropped in again at his heels, with a tail drooping discouragement, as the man swung along the creek-bed. The furrow of the old sled-trail was plainly visible, but a dozen inches of snow covered the marks of the last runners. In a month no man had come up or down that silent creek. The man held steadily on. He was not much given to thinking, and just then particularly he had nothing to think about save that he would eat lunch at the forks and that at six o'clock he would be in camp with the boys. There was nobody to talk to; and, had there been, speech would have been impossible because of the ice-muzzle on his mouth. So he continued monotonously to chew tobacco and to increase the length of his amber beard.

Once in a while the thought reiterated itself that it was very cold and that he had never experienced such cold. As he walked along he rubbed his cheek-bones and nose with the back of his mittened hand. He did this automatically, now and again changing hands. But rub as he would, the instant he stopped his cheek-bones went numb, and the following instant the end of his nose went numb. He was sure to frost his cheeks; he knew that, and experienced a pang of regret that he had not devised a nose-strap of the sort Bud wore in cold snaps. Such a strap passed across the cheeks, as well, and saved them. But it didn't matter much, after all. What were frosted cheeks? A bit painful, that was all; they were never serious.

Empty as the man's mind was of thoughts, he was keenly observant, and he noticed the changes in the creek, the curves and bends and timber-jams, and always he sharply noted where he placed his feet. Once, coming around a bend, he shied abruptly, like a startled horse, curved away from the place where he had been walking, and retreated several paces back along the trail. The creek he knew was frozen clear to the bottom,—no creek could contain water in that arctic winter,—but he knew also that there were springs that bubbled out from the hillsides and ran along under the snow and on top the ice of the creek. He knew that the coldest snaps never froze these springs, and he knew likewise their danger. They were traps. They hid pools of water under the snow that might be three inches deep, or three feet. Sometimes a skin of ice half an inch thick covered them, and in turn was covered by the snow. Sometimes there were alternate layers of water and ice-skin, so that when one broke through he kept on breaking through for a while, sometimes wetting himself to the waist.

That was why he had shied in such panic. He had felt the give under his feet and heard the crackle of a snow-hidden ice-skin. And to get his feet wet in such a temperature meant trouble and danger. At the very least it meant delay, for he would be forced to stop and build a fire, and under its protection to bare his feet while he dried his socks and moccasins. He stood and studied the creek-bed and its banks, and decided that the flow of water came from the right. He reflected awhile, rubbing his nose and cheeks, then skirted to the left, stepping gingerly and testing the footing for each step. Once clear of the danger, he took a fresh chew of tobacco and swung along at his four-mile gait.

In the course of the next two hours he came upon several similar traps. Usually the snow above the hidden pools had a sunken, candied appearance that advertised the danger. Once again, however, he had a close call; and once, suspecting danger, he compelled the dog to go on in front. The dog did not want to go. It hung back until the man shoved it forward, and then it went quickly across the white, unbroken surface. Suddenly it broke through, floundered to one side, and got away to firmer footing. It had wet its forefeet and legs, and almost immediately the water that clung to it turned to ice. It made quick efforts to lick the ice off its legs, then dropped down in the snow and began to bite out the ice that had formed between the toes. This was a matter of instinct. To permit the ice to remain would mean sore feet. It did not know this. It merely obeyed the mysterious prompting that arose from the deep crypts of its being. But the man knew, having achieved a judgment on the subject, and he removed the mitten from his right hand and helped tear out the ice-particles. He did not expose his fingers more than a minute, and was astonished at the swift numbness that smote them. It certainly was cold. He pulled on the mitten hastily, and beat the hand savagely across his chest.

At twelve o'clock the day was at its brightest. Yet the sun was too far south on its winter journey to clear the horizon. The bulge of the earth intervened between it and Henderson Creek, where the man walked under a clear sky at noon and cast no shadow. At half-past twelve, to the minute, he arrived at the forks of the creek. He was pleased at the speed he had made. If he kept it up, he would certainly be with the boys by six. He unbuttoned his jacket and shirt and drew forth his lunch. The action consumed no more than a quarter of a minute, yet in that brief moment the numbness laid hold of the exposed fingers. He did not put the mitten on, but, instead, struck the fingers a dozen sharp smashes against his leg. Then he sat down on a snow-covered log to eat. The sting that followed upon the striking of his fingers against his leg ceased so quickly that he was startled. He had had no chance to take a bite of biscuit. He struck the fingers repeatedly and returned them to the mitten, baring the other hand for the purpose of eating. He tried to take a mouthful, but the ice-muzzle prevented. He had forgotten to build a fire and thaw out. He chuckled at his foolishness, and as he chuckled he noted the numbness creeping into the exposed fingers. Also, he noted that the stinging which had first come to his toes when he sat down was already passing away. He wondered whether the toes were warm or numb. He moved them inside the moccasins and decided that they were numb.

He pulled the mitten on hurriedly and stood up. He was a bit frightened. He stamped up and down until the stinging returned into the feet. It certainly was cold, was his thought. That man from Sulphur Creek had spoken the truth when telling how cold it sometimes got in the country. And he had laughed at him at the time! That showed one must not be too sure of things. There was no mistake about it, it *was* cold. He strode up and down, stamping his feet and threshing his arms, until reassured by the returning warmth. Then he got out matches and proceeded to make a fire. From the undergrowth, where high water of the previous spring had lodged a supply of seasoned twigs, he got his fire-wood. Working carefully from a small beginning, he soon had a roaring fire, over which he thawed the ice from his face and in the protection of which he ate his biscuits. For the moment the cold of space was outwitted. The dog took satisfaction in the fire, stretching out close enough for warmth and far enough away to escape being singed.

When the man had finished, he filled his pipe and took his comfortable time over a smoke. Then he pulled on his mittens, settled the ear-flaps of his cap firmly about his ears, and took the creek trail up the left fork. The dog was disappointed and yearned back toward the fire. This man did not know cold. Possibly all the generations of his ancestry had been ignorant of cold, of real cold, of cold one hundred and seven degrees below freezing-point. But the dog knew; all its ancestry knew, and it had inherited the knowledge. And it knew that it was not good to walk abroad in such fearful cold. It was the time to lie snug in a hole in the snow and wait for a curtain of cloud to be drawn across the face of outer space whence this cold came. On the other hand, there was no keen intimacy between the dog and the man. The one was the toil-slave of the other, and the only caresses it had ever received were the caresses of the whip-lash and of harsh and menacing throat-sounds that threatened the whip-lash. So the dog made no effort to communicate its apprehension to the man. It was not concerned in the welfare of the man; it was for its own sake that it yearned back toward the fire. But the man whistled, and spoke to it with the sound of whip-lashes, and the dog swung in at the man's heels and followed after.

The man took a chew of tobacco and proceeded to start a new amber beard. Also, his moist breath quickly powdered with white his mustache, eyebrows, and lashes. There did not seem to be so many springs on the left fork of the Henderson, and for half an hour the man saw no signs of any. And then it happened. At a place where there were no signs, where the soft, unbroken snow seemed to advertise solidity beneath, the man broke through. It was not deep. He wet himself halfway to the knees before he floundered out to the firm crust.

He was angry, and cursed his luck aloud. He had hoped to get into camp with the boys at six o'clock, and this would delay him an hour, for he would have to build a fire and dry out his foot-gear. This was imperative at that low temperature—he knew that much; and he turned aside to the bank, which he climbed. On top, tangled in the underbrush about the trunks of several small spruce trees, was a high-water deposit of dry fire-wood—sticks and twigs, principally, but also larger portions of seasoned branches and fine, dry, last-year's grasses. He threw down several large pieces on top of the snow. This served for a foundation and prevented the young flame from drowning itself in the snow it otherwise would melt. The flame he got by touching a match to a small shred of birch-bark that he took from his pocket. This burned even more readily than paper. Placing it on the foundation, he fed the young flame with wisps of dry grass and with the tiniest dry twigs.

He worked slowly and carefully, keenly aware of his danger. Gradually, as the flame grew stronger, he increased the size of the twigs with which he fed it. He squatted in the snow, pulling the twigs out from their entanglement in the brush and feeding directly to the flame. He knew there must be no failure. When it is seventy-five

below zero, a man must not fail in his first attempt to build a fire—
that is, if his feet are wet. If his feet are dry, and he fails, he can run
along the trail for half a mile and restore his circulation. But the
circulation of wet and freezing feet cannot be restored by running
when it is seventy-five below. No matter how fast he runs, the wet
feet will freeze the harder.

All this the man knew. The old-timer on Sulphur Creek had told
him about it the previous fall, and now he was appreciating the advice.
Already all sensation had gone out of his feet. To build the fire he
had been forced to remove his mittens, and the fingers had quickly
gone numb. His pace of four miles an hour had kept his heart pumping
blood to the surface of his body and to all the extremities. But the
instant he stopped, the action of the pump eased down. The cold of
space smote the unprotected tip of the planet, and he, being on that
unprotected tip, received the full force of the blow. The blood of
his body recoiled before it. The blood was alive, like the dog, and
like the dog it wanted to hide away and cover itself up from the
fearful cold. So long as he walked four miles an hour, he pumped
that blood, willy-nilly, to the surface; but now it ebbed away and
sank down into the recesses of his body. The extremities were the
first to feel its absence. His wet feet froze the faster, and his exposed
fingers numbed the faster, though they had not yet begun to freeze.
Nose and cheeks were already freezing, while the skin of all his body
chilled as it lost its blood.

But he was safe. Toes and nose and cheeks would be only touched
by the frost, for the fire was beginning to burn with strength. He
was feeding it with twigs the size of his finger. In another minute he
would be able to feed it with branches the size of his wrist, and then
he could remove his wet foot-gear, and, while it dried, he could
keep his naked feet warm by the fire, rubbing them at first, of course,
with snow. The fire was a success. He was safe. He remembered the
advice of the old-timer on Sulphur Creek, and smiled. The old-timer
had been very serious in laying down the law that no man must travel
alone in the Klondike after fifty below. Well, here he was; he had
had the accident; he was alone; and he had saved himself. Those
old-timers were rather womanish, some of them, he thought. All a
man had to do was to keep his head, and he was all right. Any man
who was a man could travel alone. But it was surprising, the rapidity
with which his cheeks and nose were freezing. And he had not
thought his fingers could go lifeless in so short a time. Lifeless they
were, for he could scarcely make them move together to grip a twig,

and they seemed remote from his body and from him. When he touched a twig, he had to look and see whether or not he had hold of it. The wires were pretty well down between him and his finger-ends.

All of which counted for little. There was the fire, snapping and crackling and promising life with every dancing flame. He started to untie his moccasins. They were coated with ice; the thick German socks were like sheaths of iron halfway to the knees; and the moccasin strings were like rods of steel all twisted and knotted as by some conflagration. For a moment he tugged with his numb fingers, then, realizing the folly of it, he drew his sheath-knife.

But before he could cut the strings, it happened. It was his own fault or, rather, his mistake. He should not have built the fire under the spruce tree. He should have built it in the open. But it had been easier to pull the twigs from the brush and drop them directly on the fire. Now the tree under which he had done this carried a weight of snow on its boughs. No wind had blown for weeks, and each bough was fully freighted. Each time he had pulled a twig he had communicated a slight agitation to the tree—an imperceptible agitation, so far as he was concerned, but an agitation sufficient to bring about the disaster. High up in the tree one bough capsized its load of snow. This fell on the boughs beneath, capsizing them. This process continued, spreading out and involving the whole tree. It grew like an avalanche, and it descended without warning upon the man and the fire, and the fire was blotted out! Where it had burned was a mantle of fresh and disordered snow.

The man was shocked. It was as though he had just heard his own sentence of death. For a moment he sat and stared at the spot where the fire had been. Then he grew very calm. Perhaps the old-timer on Sulphur Creek was right. If he had only had a trail-mate he would have been in no danger now. The trail-mate could have built the fire. Well, it was up to him to build the fire over again, and this second time there must be no failure. Even if he succeeded, he would most likely lose some toes. His feet must be badly frozen by now, and there would be some time before the second fire was ready.

Such were his thoughts, but he did not sit and think them. He was busy all the time they were passing through his mind. He made a new foundation for a fire, this time in the open, where no treacherous tree could blot it out. Next, he gathered dry grasses and tiny twigs from the high-water flotsam. He could not bring his fingers together to pull them out, but he was able to gather them by the handful. In this way he got many rotten twigs and bits of green moss that were undesirable, but it was the best he could do. He worked methodically, even collecting an armful of the larger branches to be used later when the fire gathered strength. And all the while the dog sat and watched him, a certain yearning wistfulness in its eyes, for it looked upon him as the fire-provider, and the fire was slow in coming.

When all was ready, the man reached in his pocket for a second piece of birch-bark. He knew the bark was there, and, though he could not feel it with his fingers, he could hear its crisp rustling as he fumbled for it. Try as he would, he could not clutch hold of it. And all the time, in his consciousness, was the knowledge that each instant his feet were freezing. This thought tended to put him in a panic, but he fought against it and kept calm. He pulled on his mittens with his teeth, and threshed his arms back and forth, beating his hands with all his might against his sides. He did this sitting down, and he stood up to do it; and all the while the dog sat in the snow, its wolf-brush of a tail curled around warmly over its forefeet, its sharp wolf-ears pricked forward intently as it watched the man. And the man, as he beat and threshed with his arms and hands, felt a great surge of envy as he regarded the creature that was warm and secure in its natural covering.

After a time he was aware of the first faraway signals of sensation in his beaten fingers. The faint tingling grew stronger till it evolved into a stinging ache that was excruciating, but which the man hailed with satisfaction. He stripped the mitten from his right hand and fetched forth the birch-bark. The exposed fingers were quickly going numb again. Next he brought out his bunch of sulphur matches. But the tremendous cold had already driven the life out of his fingers. In his effort to separate one match from the others, the whole bunch fell in the snow. He tried to pick it out of the snow, but failed. The dead fingers could neither touch nor clutch. He was very careful. He drove the thought of his freezing feet, and nose, and cheeks, out of his mind, devoting his whole soul to the matches. He watched, using the sense of vision in place of that of touch, and when he saw his fingers on each side of the bunch, he closed them—that is, he willed to close them, for the wires were down, and the fingers did not obey. He pulled the mitten on the right hand, and beat it fiercely against his knee. Then, with both mittened hands, he scooped the bunch of matches, along with much snow, into his lap. Yet he was no better off.

After some manipulation he managed to get the bunch between the heels of his mittened hands. In this fashion he carried it to his mouth. The ice crackled and snapped when by a violent effort he opened his mouth. He drew the lower jaw in, curled the upper lip out of the way, and scraped the bunch with his upper teeth in order to separate a match. He succeeded in getting one, which he dropped on his lap. He was no better off. He could not pick it up. Then he devised a way. He picked it up in his teeth and scratched it on his leg. Twenty times he scratched before he succeeded in lighting it. As it flamed he held it with his teeth to the birch-bark. But the burning brimstone went up his nostrils and into his lungs, causing him to cough spasmodically. The match fell into the snow and went out.

The old-timer on Sulphur Creek was right, he thought in the moment of controlled despair that ensued: after fifty below, a man should travel with a partner. He beat his hands, but failed in exciting any sensation. Suddenly he bared both hands, removing the mittens with his teeth. He caught the whole bunch between the heels of his hands. His arm-muscles not being frozen enabled him to press the hand-heels tightly against the matches. Then he scratched the bunch along his leg. It flared into flame, seventy sulphur matches at once! There was no wind to blow them out. He kept his head to one side to escape the strangling fumes, and held the blazing bunch to the birch-bark. As he so held it, he became aware of sensation in his hand. His flesh was burning. He could smell it. Deep down below the surface he could feel it. The sensation developed into pain that grew acute. And still he endured it, holding the flame of the matches clumsily to the bark that would not light readily because his own burning hands were in the way, absorbing most of the flame.

At last, when he could endure no more, he jerked his hands apart. The blazing matches fell sizzling into the snow, but the birch-bark was alight. He began laying dry grasses and the tiniest twigs on the flame. He could not pick and choose, for he had to lift the fuel between the heels of his hands. Small pieces of rotten wood and green moss clung to the twigs, and he bit them off as well as he could with his teeth. He cherished the flame carefully and awkwardly. It meant life, and it must not perish. The withdrawal of blood from the surface of his body now made him begin to shiver, and he grew more awkward. A large piece of green moss fell squarely on the little fire. He tried to poke it out with his fingers, but his shivering frame made him poke too far, and he disrupted the nucleus of the little fire, the burning grasses and tiny twigs separating and scattering. He tried to poke them together again, but in spite of the tenseness of the effort, his shivering got away with him, and the twigs were hopelessly scattered. Each twig gushed a puff of smoke and went out. The fire-provider had failed. As he looked apathetically about him, his eyes chanced on the dog, sitting across the ruins of the fire from him, in the snow, making restless, hunching movements, slightly lifting one forefoot and then the other, shifting its weight back and forth on them with wistful eagerness.

The sight of the dog put a wild idea into his head. He remembered the tale of the man, caught in a blizzard, who killed a steer and crawled inside the carcass, and so was saved. He would kill the dog and bury his hands in the warm body until the numbness went out of them. Then he could build another fire. He spoke to the dog, calling it to him; but in his voice was a strange note of fear that frightened the animal, who had never known the man to speak in such way before. Something was the matter, and its suspicious nature sensed danger—it knew not what danger, but somewhere, somehow, in its brain arose an apprehension of the man. It flattened its ears down at the sound of the man's voice, and its restless, hunching movements and the liftings and shiftings of its forefeet became more pronounced; but it would not come to the man. He got on his hands and knees and crawled toward the dog. This unusual posture again excited suspicion, and the animal sidled mincingly away.

The man sat up in the snow for a moment and struggled for calmness. Then he pulled on his mittens, by means of his teeth, and got upon his feet. He glanced down at first in order to assure himself that he was really standing up, for the absence of sensation in his feet left him unrelated to the earth. His erect position in itself started to drive the webs of suspicion from the dog's mind; and when he spoke peremptorily, with the sound of whip-lashes in his voice, the dog rendered its customary allegiance and came to him. As it came within reaching distance, the man lost his control. His arms flashed out to the dog, and he experienced genuine surprise when he discovered that his hands could not clutch, that there was neither bend nor feeling in the fingers. He had forgotten for the moment that they were frozen and that they were freezing more and more. All this happened quickly, and before the animal could get away, he encircled its body with his arms. He sat down in the snow, and in this fashion held the dog, while it snarled and whined and struggled.

But it was all he could do, hold its body encircled in his arms and sit there. He realized that he could not kill the dog. There was no way to do it. With his helpless hands he could neither draw nor hold his sheath-knife nor throttle the animal. He released it, and it plunged wildly away, with tail between its legs, and still snarling. It halted forty feet away and surveyed him curiously, with ears sharply pricked forward. The man looked down at his hands in order to locate them, and found them hanging on the ends of his arms. It struck him as curious that one should have to use his eyes in order to find out where his hands were. He began threshing his arms back and forth, beating the mittened hands against his sides. He did this for five minutes, violently, and his heart pumped enough blood up to the surface to put a stop to his shivering. But no sensation was aroused in the hands. He had an impression that they hung like weights on the ends of his arms, but when he tried to run the impression down, he could not find it.

A certain fear of death, dull and oppressive, came to him. This fear quickly became poignant as he realized that it was no longer a mere matter of freezing his fingers and toes, or of losing his hands and feet, but that it was a matter of life and death with the chances against him. This threw him into a panic, and he turned and ran up the creek-bed along the old, dim trail. The dog joined in behind and kept up with him. He ran blindly, without intention, in fear such as he had never known in his life. Slowly, as he ploughed and floundered through the snow, he began to see things again,—the banks of the creek, the old timber-jams, the leafless aspens, and the sky. The running made him feel better. He did not shiver. Maybe, if he ran on, his feet would thaw out; and, anyway, if he ran far enough, he would reach camp and the boys. Without doubt he would lose some fingers and toes and some of his face; but the boys would take care of him, and save the rest of him when he got there. And at the same time there was another thought in his mind that said he would never get to the camp and the boys; that it was too many miles away, that the freezing had too great a start on him, and that he would soon be stiff and dead. This thought he kept in the background and refused to consider. Sometimes it pushed itself forward and demanded to be heard, but he thrust it back and strove to think of other things.

It struck him as curious that he could run at all on feet so frozen that he could not feel them when they struck the earth and took the weight of his body. He seemed to himself to skim along above the surface, and to have no connection with the earth. Somewhere he had once seen a winged Mercury, and he wondered if Mercury felt as he felt when skimming over the earth.

His theory of running until he reached camp and the boys had one flaw in it: he lacked the endurance. Several times he stumbled, and finally he tottered, crumpled up, and fell. When he tried to rise, he failed. He must sit and rest, he decided, and next time he would merely walk and keep on going. As he sat and regained his breath, he noted that he was feeling quite warm and comfortable. He was not shivering, and it even seemed that a warm glow had come to his chest and trunk. And yet, when he touched his nose or cheeks, there was no sensation. Running would not thaw them out. Nor would it thaw out his hands and feet. Then the thought came to him that the frozen portions of his body must be extending. He tried to keep this thought down, to forget it, to think of something else; he was aware of the panicky feeling that it caused, and he was afraid of the panic. But the thought asserted itself, and persisted, until it produced a vision of his body totally frozen. This was too much, and he made another wild run along the trail. Once he slowed down to a walk, but the thought of the freezing extending itself made him run again.

And all the time the dog ran with him, at his heels. When he fell down a second time, it curled its tail over its forefeet and sat in front of him, facing him, curiously eager and intent. The warmth and security of the animal angered him, and he cursed it till it flattened down its ears appeasingly. This time the shivering came more quickly upon the man. He was losing in his battle with the frost. It was creeping into his body from all sides. The thought of it drove him on, but he ran no more than a hundred feet, when he staggered and pitched headlong. It was his last panic. When he had recovered his breath and control, he sat up and entertained in his mind the conception of meeting death with dignity. However, the conception did not come to him in such terms. His idea of it was that he had been making a fool of himself, running around like a chicken with its head cut off—such was the simile that occurred to him. Well, he was bound to freeze anyway, and he might as well take it decently. With this new-found peace of mind came the first glimmerings of drowsiness. A good idea, he thought, to sleep off to death. It was like taking an anæsthetic. Freezing was not so bad as people thought. There were lots worse ways to die.

He pictured the boys finding his body next day. Suddenly he found himself with them, coming along the trail and looking for himself. And, still with them, he came around a turn in the trail and found himself lying in the snow. He did not belong with himself any more, for even then he was out of himself, standing with the boys and looking at himself in the snow. It certainly was cold, was his thought. When he got back to the States he could tell the folks what real cold was. He drifted on from this to a vision of the old-timer on Sulphur Creek. He could see him quite clearly, warm and comfortable, and smoking a pipe.

"You were right, old hoss; you were right," the man mumbled to the old-timer of Sulphur Creek.

Then the man drowsed off into what seemed to him the most comfortable and satisfying sleep he had ever known. The dog sat facing him and waiting. The brief day drew to a close in a long, slow twilight. There were no signs of a fire to be made, and, besides, never in the dog's experience had it known a man to sit like that in the snow and make no fire. As the twilight drew on, its eager yearning for the fire mastered it, and with a great lifting and shifting of forefeet, it whined softly, then flattened its ears down in anticipation of being chidden by the man. But the man remained silent. Later, the dog whined loudly. And still later it crept close to the man and caught the scent of death. This made the animal bristle and back away. A little longer it delayed, howling under the stars that leaped and danced and shone brightly in the cold sky. Then it turned and trotted up the trail in the direction of the camp it knew, where were the other food-providers and fire-providers.

THE CABALLERO'S WAY

O. Henry

THE CISCO KID had killed six men in more or less fair scrimmages, had murdered twice as many (mostly Mexicans), and had winged a larger number whom he modestly forbore to count. Therefore a woman loved him.

The Kid was twenty-five, looked twenty; and a careful insurance company would have estimated the probable time of his demise at, say, twenty-six. His habitat was anywhere between the Frio and the Rio Grande. He killed for the love of it—because he was quick-tempered—to avoid arrest—for his own amusement—any reason that came to his mind would suffice. He had escaped capture because he could shoot five-sixths of a second sooner than any sheriff or ranger in the service, and because he rode a speckled roan horse that knew every cow-path in the mesquite and pear thickets from San Antonio to Matamoras.

Tonia Perez, the girl who loved the Cisco Kid, was half Carmen, half Madonna, and the rest—oh, yes, a woman who is half Carmen and half Madonna can always be something more—the rest, let us say, was humming-bird. She lived in a grass-roofed *jacal* near a little Mexican settlement at the Lone Wolf Crossing of the Frio. With her lived a father or grandfather, a lineal Aztec, somewhat less than a thousand years old, who herded a hundred goats and lived in a continuous drunken dream from drinking *mescal*. Back of the *jacal* a tremendous forest of bristling pear, twenty feet high at its worst, crowded almost to its door. It was along the bewildering maze of this spinous thicket that the speckled roan would bring the Kid to see his girl. And once, clinging like a lizard to the ridge-pole, high up under the peaked grass roof, he had heard Tonia, with her Madonna face and Carmen

35

beauty and humming-bird soul, parley with the sheriff's posse, denying knowledge of her man in her soft *mélange* of Spanish and English.

One day the adjutant-general of the State, who is, *ex officio,* commander of the ranger forces, wrote some sarcastic lines to Captain Duval of Company X, stationed at Laredo, relative to the serene and undisturbed existence led by murderers and desperadoes in the said captain's territory.

The captain turned the colour of brick dust under his tan, and forwarded the letter, after adding a few comments, per ranger Private Bill Adamson, to ranger Lieutenant Sandridge, camped at a water hole on the Nueces with a squad of five men in preservation of law and order.

Lieutenant Sandridge turned a beautiful *couleur de rose* through his ordinary strawberry complexion, tucked the letter in his hip pocket, and chewed off the ends of his gamboge moustache.

The next morning he saddled his horse and rode alone to the Mexican settlement at the Lone Wolf Crossing of the Frio, twenty miles away.

Six feet two, blond as a Viking, quiet as a deacon, dangerous as a machine gun, Sandridge moved among the *Jacales,* patiently seeking news of the Cisco Kid.

Far more than the law, the Mexicans dreaded the cold and certain vengeance of the lone rider that the ranger sought. It had been one of the Kid's pastimes to shoot Mexicans "to see them kick": if he demanded from them moribund Terpsichorean feats, simply that he might be entertained, what terrible and extreme penalties would be certain to follow should they anger him! One and all they lounged with upturned palms and shrugging shoulders, filling the air with "*quien sabes*" and denials of the Kid's acquaintance.

But there was a man named Fink who kept a store at the Crossing—a man of many nationalities, tongues, interests, and ways of thinking.

"No use to ask them Mexicans," he said to Sandridge. "They're afraid to tell. This *hombre* they call the Kid—Goodall is his name, ain't it?—he's been in my store once or twice. I have an idea you might run across him at—but I guess I don't keer to say, myself. I'm two seconds later in pulling a gun than I used to be, and the difference is worth thinking about. But this Kid's got a half-Mexican girl at the Crossing that he comes to see. She lives in that *jacal* a hundred yards down the arroyo at the edge of the pear. Maybe she—no, I don't suppose she would, but that *jacal* would be a good place to watch, anyway."

Sandridge rode down to the *jacal* of Perez. The sun was low, and the broad shade of the great pear thicket already covered the grass-thatched hut. The goats were enclosed for the night in a brush corral near by. A few kids walked the top of it, nibbling the chaparral leaves. The old Mexican lay upon a blanket on the grass, already in a stupor from his mescal, and dreaming, perhaps, of the nights when he and Pizarro touched glasses to their New World fortunes—so old his wrinkled face seemed to proclaim him to be. And in the door of the *jacal* stood Tonia. And Lieutenant Sandridge sat in his saddle staring at her like a gannet agape at a sailorman.

The Cisco Kid was a vain person, as all eminent and successful assassins are, and his bosom would have been ruffled had he known that at a simple exchange of glances two persons, in whose minds he had been looming large, suddenly abandoned (at least for the time) all thought of him.

Never before had Tonia seen such a man as this. He seemed to be made of sunshine and blood-red tissue and clear weather. He seemed to illuminate the shadow of the pear when he smiled, as though the sun were rising again. The men she had known had been small and dark. Even the Kid, in spite of his achievements, was a stripling no larger than herself, with black, straight hair and a cold, marble face that chilled the noonday.

As for Tonia, though she sends description to the poorhouse, let her make a millionaire of your fancy. Her blue-black hair, smoothly divided in the middle and bound close to her head, and her large eyes full of the Latin melancholy, gave her the Madonna touch. Her motions and air spoke of the concealed fire and the desire to charm that she had inherited from the *gitanas* of the Basque province. As for the humming-bird part of her, that dwelt in her heart; you could not perceive it unless her bright red skirt and dark blue blouse gave you a symbolic hint of the vagarious bird.

The newly lighted sun-god asked for a drink of water. Tonia brought it from the red jar hanging under the brush shelter. Sandridge considered it necessary to dismount so as to lessen the trouble of her ministrations.

I play no spy; nor do I assume to master the thoughts of any human heart; but I assert, by the chronicler's right, that before a quarter of an hour had sped, Sandridge was teaching her how to plait a six-strand rawhide stake-rope, and Tonia had explained to him that were it not for her little English book that the peripatetic *padre* had given her and the little crippled *chivo,* that she fed from a bottle, she would be very, very lonely indeed.

Which leads to a suspicion that the Kid's fences needed repairing, and that the adjutant-general's sarcasm had fallen upon unproductive soil.

In his camp by the water hole Lieutenant Sandridge announced and reiterated his intention of either causing the Cisco Kid to nibble the black loam of the Frio country prairies or of haling him before a judge and jury. That sounded business-like. Twice a week he rode over to the Lone Wolf Crossing of the Frio, and directed Tonia's slim, slightly lemon-tinted fingers among the intricacies of the slowly growing lariata. A six-strand plait is hard to learn and easy to teach.

The ranger knew that he might find the Kid there at any visit. He kept his armament ready, and had a frequent eye for the pear thicket at the rear of the *jacal.* Thus he might bring down the kite and the humming-bird with one stone.

While the sunny-haired ornithologist was pursuing his studies the Cisco Kid was also attending to his professional duties. He moodily shot up a saloon in a small cow village on Quintana Creek, killed the town marshal (plugging him neatly in the centre of his tin badge), and then rode away, morose and unsatisfied. No true artist is uplifted by shooting an aged man carrying an old-style .38 bulldog.

On his way the Kid suddenly experienced the yearning that all men feel when wrong-doing loses its keen edge of delight. He yearned for the woman he loved to reassure him that she was his in spite of it. He wanted her to call his bloodthirstiness bravery and his cruelty devotion. He wanted Tonia to bring him water from the red jar under the brush shelter, and tell him how the *chivo* was thriving on the bottle.

The Kid turned the speckled roan's head up the ten-mile pear flat that stretches along the Arroyo Hondo until it ends at the Lone Wolf Crossing of the Frio. The roan whickered; for he had a sense of locality and direction equal to that of a belt-line street-car horse; and he knew he would soon be nibbling the rich mesquite grass at the end of a forty-foot stake-rope while Ulysses rested his head in Circe's straw-roofed hut.

More weird and lonesome than the journey of an Amazonian explorer is the ride of one through a Texas pear flat. With dismal monotony and startling variety the uncanny and multiform shapes of the cacti lift their twisted trunks, and fat, bristly hands to encumber the way. The demon plant, appearing to live without soil or rain, seems to taunt the parched traveller with its lush grey greenness. It warps itself a thousand times about what look to be open and inviting paths, only to lure the rider into blind and impassable spine-defended "bottoms of the bag," leaving him to retreat, if he can, with the points of the compass whirling in his head.

To be lost in the pear is to die almost the death of the thief on the cross, pierced by nails and with grotesque shapes of all the fiends hovering about.

But it was not so with the Kid and his mount. Winding, twisting, circling, tracing the most fantastic and bewildering trail ever picked out, the good roan lessened the distance to the Lone Wolf Crossing with every coil and turn that he made.

While they fared the Kid sang. He knew but one tune and sang it, as he knew but one code and lived it, and but one girl and loved her. He was a single-minded man of conventional ideas. He had a voice like a coyote with bronchitis, but whenever he chose to sing his song he sang it. It was a conventional song of the camps and trail, running at its beginning as near as may be to these words:

> Don't you monkey with my Lulu girl
> Or I'll tell you what I'll do—

and so on. The roan was inured to it, and did not mind.

But even the poorest singer will, after a certain time, gain his own consent to refrain from contributing to the world's noises. So the Kid, by the time he was within a mile or two of Tonia's *jacal,* had reluctantly allowed his song to die away—not because his vocal performance had become less charming to his own ears, but because his laryngeal muscles were aweary.

As though he were in a circus ring the speckled roan wheeled and danced through the labyrinth of pear until at length his rider knew by certain landmarks that the Lone Wolf Crossing was close at hand. Then, where the pear was thinner, he caught sight of the grass roof of the *jacal* and the hackberry tree on the edge of the arroyo. A few yards farther the Kid stopped the roan and gazed intently through the prickly openings. Then he dismounted, dropped the roan's reins, and proceeded on foot, stooping and silent, like an Indian. The roan, knowing his part, stood still, making no sound.

The Kid crept noiselessly to the very edge of the pear thicket and reconnoitered between the leaves of a clump of cactus.

Ten yards from his hiding-place, in the shade of the *jacal,* sat his Tonia calmly plaiting a rawhide lariat. So far she might surely escape condemnation; women have been known, from time to time, to engage in more mischievous occupations. But if all must be told, there is to be added that her head reposed against the broad and comfortable chest of a tall red-and-yellow man, and that his arm was about her, guiding her nimble small fingers that required so many lessons at the intricate six-strand plait.

Sandridge glanced quickly at the dark mass of pear when he heard a slight squeaking sound that was not altogether unfamiliar. A gun-scabbard will make that sound when one grasps the handle of a six-shooter suddenly. But the sound was not repeated; and Tonia's fingers needed close attention.

And then, in the shadow of death, they began to talk of their love; and in the still July afternoon every word they uttered reached the ears of the Kid.

"Remember, then," said Tonia, "you must not come again until I send for you. Soon he will be here. A *vaquero* at the *tienda* said to-day he saw him on the Guadalupe three days ago. When he is that near he always comes. If he comes and finds you here he will kill you. So, for my sake, you must come no more until I send you the word."

"All right," said the ranger. "And then what?"

"And then," said the girl, "you must bring your men here and kill him. If not, he will kill you."

"He ain't a man to surrender, that's sure," said Sandridge. "It's kill or be killed for the officer that goes up against Mr. Cisco Kid."

"He must die," said the girl. "Otherwise there will not be any peace in the world for thee and me. He has killed many. Let him so die. Bring your men, and give him no chance to escape."

"You used to think right much of him," said Sandridge.

Tonia dropped the lariat, twisted herself around, and curved a lemon-tinted arm over the ranger's shoulder.

"But then," she murmured in liquid Spanish, "I had not beheld thee, thou great, red mountain of a man! And thou art kind and good, as well as strong. Could one choose him, knowing thee? Let him die; for then I will not be filled with fear by day and night lest he hurt thee or me."

"How can I know when he comes?" asked Sandridge.

"When he comes," said Tonia, "he remains two days, sometimes three. Gregorio, the small son of old Luisa, the *lavandera,* has a swift pony. I will write a letter to thee and send it by him, saying how it will be best to come upon him. By Gregorio will the letter come. And bring many men with thee, and have much care, oh, dear red one, for the rattlesnake is not quicker to strike than is '*El Chivato*,' as they call him, to send a ball from his *pistola*."

"The Kid's handy with his gun, sure enough," admitted Sandridge, "but when I come for him I shall come alone. I'll get him by myself or not at all. The Cap wrote one or two things to me that make me want to do the trick without any help. You let me know when Mr. Kid arrives, and I'll do the rest."

"I will send you the message by the boy Gregorio," said the girl. "I knew you were braver than that small slayer of men who never smiles. How could I ever have thought I cared for him?"

It was time for the ranger to ride back to his camp on the water hole. Before he mounted his horse he raised the slight form of Tonia with one arm high from the earth for a parting salute. The drowsy stillness of the torpid summer air still lay thick upon the dreaming afternoon. The smoke from the fire in the *jacal*, where the *frijoles* blubbered in the iron pot, rose straight as a plumb-line above the clay-daubed chimney. No sound or movement disturbed the serenity of the dense pear thicket ten yards away.

When the form of Sandridge had disappeared, loping his big dun down the steep banks of the Frio crossing, the Kid crept back to his own horse, mounted him, and rode back along the tortuous trail he had come.

But not far. He stopped and waited in the silent depths of the pear until half an hour had passed. And then Tonia heard the high, untrue notes of his unmusical singing coming nearer and nearer; and she ran to the edge of the pear to meet him.

The Kid seldom smiled; but he smiled and waved his hat when he saw her. He dismounted, and his girl sprang into his arms. The Kid looked at her fondly. His thick, black hair clung to his head like a wrinkled mat. The meeting brought a slight ripple of some under-current of feeling to his smooth, dark face that was usually as motionless as a clay mask.

"How's my girl?" he asked, holding her close.

"Sick of waiting so long for you, dear one," she answered. "My eyes are dim with always gazing into that devil's pincushion through which you come. And I can see into it such a little way, too. But you are here, beloved one, and I will not scold. *Que mal muchacho!* not to come to see your *alma* more often. Go in and rest, and let me water your horse and stake him with the long rope. There is cool water in the jar for you."

The Kid kissed her affectionately.

"Not if the court knows itself do I let a lady stake my horse for me," said he. "But if you'll run in, *chica,* and throw a pot of coffee together while I attend to the *caballo,* I'll be a good deal obliged."

Besides his marksmanship the Kid had another attribute for which he admired himself greatly. He was *muy caballero,* as the Mexicans express it, where the ladies were concerned. For them he had always gentle words and consideration. He could not have spoken a harsh word to a woman. He might ruthlessly slay their husbands and brothers, but he could not have laid the weight of a finger in anger upon a woman. Wherefore many of that interesting division of humanity who had come under the spell of his politeness declared their disbelief in the stories circulated about Mr. Kid. One shouldn't believe everything one heard, they said. When confronted by their indignant men folk with proof of the *caballero's* deeds of infamy, they said maybe he had been driven to it, and that he knew how to treat a lady, anyhow.

Considering this extremely courteous idiosyncrasy of the Kid and the pride that he took in it, one can perceive that the solution of the problem that was presented to him by what he saw and heard from his hiding-place in the pear that afternoon (at least as to one of the actors) must have been obscured by difficulties. And yet one could not think of the Kid overlooking little matters of that kind.

At the end of the short twilight they gathered around a supper of *frijoles,* goat steaks, canned peaches, and coffee, by the light of a lantern in the *jacal.* Afterward, the ancestor, his flock corralled, smoked a cigarette and became a mummy in a grey blanket. Tonia washed the few dishes while the Kid dried them with the flour-sacking towel. Her eyes shone; she chatted volubly of the inconsequent happenings of her small world since the Kid's last visit; it was as all his other home-comings had been.

Then outside Tonia swung in a grass hammock with her guitar and sang sad *canciones de amor.*

"Do you love me just the same, old girl?" asked the Kid, hunting for his cigarette papers.

"Always the same, little one," said Tonia, her dark eyes lingering upon him.

"I must go over to Fink's," said the Kid, rising, "for some tobacco. I thought I had another sack in my coat. I'll be back in a quarter of an hour."

"Hasten," said Tonia, "and tell me—how long shall I call you my own this time? Will you be gone again to-morrow, leaving me to grieve, or will you be longer with your Tonia?"

"Oh, I might stay two or three days this trip," said the Kid, yawning. "I've been on the dodge for a month, and I'd like to rest up."

He was gone half an hour for his tobacco. When he returned Tonia was still lying in the hammock.

"It's funny," said the Kid, "how I feel. I feel like there was somebody lying behind every bush and tree waiting to shoot me. I never had mullygrubs like them before. Maybe it's one of them presumptions. I've got half a notion to light out in the morning before day. The Guadalupe country is burning up about that old Dutchman I plugged down there."

"You are not afraid—no one could make my brave little one fear."

"Well, I haven't been usually regarded as a jack-rabbit when it comes to scrapping; but I don't want a posse smoking me out when I'm in your *jacal*. Somebody might get hurt that oughtn't to."

"Remain with your Tonia; no one will find you here."

The Kid looked keenly into the shadows up and down the arroyo and toward the dim lights of the Mexican village.

"I'll see how it looks later on," was his decision.

At midnight a horseman rode into the rangers' camp, blazing his way by noisy "halloes" to indicate a pacific mission. Sandridge and one or two others turned out to investigate the row. The rider announced himself to be Domingo Sales, from the Lone Wolf Crossing. He bore a letter for Señor Sandridge. Old Luisa, the *lavandera,* had persuaded him to bring it, he said, her son Gregorio being too ill of a fever to ride.

Sandridge lighted the camp lantern and read the letter. These were its words:

Dear One: He has come. Hardly had you ridden away when he came out of the pear. When he first talked he said he would stay three days or more. Then as it grew later he was like a wolf or a fox, and walked about without rest, looking and listening. Soon he said he must leave before daylight when it is dark and stillest. And then he seemed to suspect that I be not true to him. He looked at me so strange that I am frightened. I swear to him that I love him, his own Tonia. Last of all he said I must prove to him I am true. He thinks that even now men are waiting to kill him as he rides from my house. To escape he says he will dress in my clothes, my red skirt and the blue waist I wear and the brown mantilla over the head, and thus ride away.

But before that he says that I must put on his clothes, his *pantalones* and *camisa* and hat, and ride away on his horse from the *jacal* as far as the big road beyond the crossing and back again. This before he goes, so he can tell if I am true and if men are hidden to shoot him. It is a terrible thing. An hour before daybreak this is to be. Come, my dear one, and kill this man and take me for your Tonia. Do not try to take hold of him alive, but kill him quickly. Knowing all, you should do that. You must come long before the time and hide yourself in the little shed near the *jacal* where the wagon and saddles are kept. It is dark in there. He will wear my red skirt and blue waist and brown mantilla. I send you a hundred kisses. Come surely and shoot quickly and straight.

THINE OWN TONIA.

Sandridge quickly explained to his men the official part of the missive. The rangers protested against his going alone.

"I'll get him easy enough," said the lieutenant. "The girl's got him trapped. And don't even think he'll get the drop on me."

Sandridge saddled his horse and rode to the Lone Wolf Crossing. He tied his big dun in a clump of brush on the arroyo, took his Winchester from its scabbard, and carefully approached the Perez *jacal*. There was only the half of a high moon drifted over by ragged, milk-white gulf clouds.

The wagon-shed was an excellent place for ambush; and the ranger got inside it safely. In the black shadow of the brush shelter in front of the *jacal* he could see a horse tied and hear him impatiently pawing the hard-trodden earth.

He waited almost an hour before two figures came out of the *jacal*. One, in man's clothes, quickly mounted the horse and galloped past the wagon-shed toward the crossing and village. And then the other figure, in skirt, waist, and mantilla over its head, stepped out into the faint moonlight, gazing after the rider. Sandridge thought he would take his chance then before Tonia rode back. He fancied she might not care to see it.

"Throw up your hands," he ordered loudly, stepping out of the wagon-shed with his Winchester at his shoulder.

There was a quick turn of the figure, but no movement to obey, so the ranger pumped in the bullets—one—two—three—and then twice more; for you never could be too sure of bringing down the Cisco Kid. There was no danger of missing at ten paces, even in that half moonlight.

The old ancestor, asleep on his blanket, was awakened by the shots. Listening further, he heard a great cry from some man in mortal distress or anguish, and rose up grumbling at the disturbing ways of moderns.

The tall, red ghost of a man burst into the *jacal,* reaching one hand, shaking like a *tule* reed, for the lantern hanging on its nail. The other spread a letter on the table.

"Look at this letter, Perez," cried the man. "Who wrote it?"

"*Ah, Dios!* it is Señor Sandridge," mumbled the old man, approaching. "*Pues, señor,* that letter was written by '*El Chivato,*' as he is called—by the man of Tonia. They say he is a bad man; I do not know. While Tonia slept he wrote the letter and sent it by this old hand of mine to Domingo Sales to be brought to you. Is there anything wrong in the letter? I am very old; and I did not know. *Valgame Dios!* it is a very foolish world; and there is nothing in the house to drink—nothing to drink."

Just then all that Sandridge could think of to do was to go outside and throw himself face downward in the dust by the side of his humming-bird, of whom not a feather fluttered. He was not a *caballero* by instinct, and he could not understand the niceties of revenge.

A mile away the rider who had ridden past the wagon-shed struck up a harsh, untuneful song, the words of which began:

Don't you monkey with my Lulu girl
Or I'll tell you what I'll do—

THE SEED FROM THE SEPULCHRE

Clark Ashton Smith

"Yes, I found the place," said Falmer. "It's a queer sort of place, pretty much as the legends describe it." He spat quickly into the fire, as if the act of speech had been physically distasteful to him, and, half averting his face from the scrutiny of Thone, stared with morose and somber eyes into the jungle-matted Venezuelan darkness.

Thone, still weak and dizzy from the fever that had incapacitated him for continuing their journey to its end, was curiously puzzled. Falmer, he thought, had under-gone an inexplicable change during the three days of his absence; a change that was too elusive in some of its phases to be fully defined or delimited.

Other phases, however, were all too obvious. Falmer, even during extreme hardship or illness, had heretofore been unquenchably loquacious and cheerful. Now he seemed sullen, uncommunicative, as if preoccupied with far-off things of disagreeable import. His bluff face had grown hollow—even pointed—and his eyes had narrowed to secretive slits. Thone was troubled by these changes, though he tried to dismiss his impressions as mere distempered fancies due to the influence of the ebbing fever.

"But can't you tell me what the place was like?," he persisted.

"There isn't much to tell," said Falmer, in a queer grumbling tone. "Just a few crumbling walls and falling pillars."

"But didn't you find the burial-pit of the Indian legend, where the gold was supposed to be?"

"I found it—but there was no treasure." Falmer's voice had taken on a forbidding surliness; and Thone decided to refrain from further questioning.

"I guess," he commented lightly, "that we had better stick to orchid hunting. Treasure trove doesn't seem to be in our line. By the way, did you see any unusual flowers or plants during the trip?"

"Hell, no," Falmer snapped. His face had gone suddenly ashen in the firelight, and his eyes had assumed a set glare that might have meant either fear or anger. "Shut up, can't you? I don't want to talk. I've had a headache all day; some damned Venezuelan fever coming on, I suppose. We'd better head for the Orinoco tomorrow. I've had all I want of this trip."

James Falmer and Roderick Thone, professional orchid hunters, with two Indian guides, had been following an obscure tributary of the upper Orinoco. The country was rich in rare flowers; and, beyond its floral wealth, they had been drawn by vague but persistent rumors among the local tribes concerning the existence of a ruined city somewhere on this tributary; a city that contained a burial pit in which vast treasures of gold, silver, and jewels had been interred together with the dead of some nameless people. The two men had thought it worthwhile to investigate these rumors. Thone had fallen sick while they were still a full day's journey from the site of the ruins, and Falmer had gone on in a canoe with one of the Indians, leaving the other to attend to Thone. He had returned at nightfall of the third day following his departure.

Thone decided after a while, as he lay staring at his companion, that the latter's taciturnity and moroseness were perhaps due to disappointment over his failure to find the treasure. It must have been that, together with some tropical infection working in the man's blood. However, he admitted doubtfully to himself, it was not like Falmer to be disappointed or downcast under such circumstances. Falmer did not speak again, but sat glaring before him as if he saw something invisible to others beyond the labyrinth of fire-touched boughs and lianas in which the whispering, stealthy darkness crouched. Somehow, there was a shadowy fear in his aspect. Thone continued to watch him, and saw that the Indians, impassive and cryptic, were also watching him, as if with some obscure expectancy. The riddle was too much for Thone, and he gave it up after a while, lapsing into restless, fever-turbulent slumber from which he awakened at intervals, to see the set face of Falmer, dimmer and more distorted each time with the slowly dying fire and the invading shadows.

Thone felt stronger in the morning: his brain was clear, his pulse tranquil once more; and he saw with mounting concern the indisposition of Falmer, who seemed to rouse and exert himself with great difficulty, speaking hardly a word and moving with singular stiffness and sluggishness. He appeared to have forgotten his announced project of returning toward the Orinoco, and Thone took entire charge of the preparations for departure. His companion's condition puzzled him more and more—apparently there was no fever and the symptoms were wholly ambiguous. However, on general principles, he administered a stiff dose of quinine to Falmer before they started.

The paling saffron of sultry dawn sifted upon them through the jungle tops as they loaded their belongings into the dugouts and pushed off down the slow current. Thone sat near the bow of one of the boats, with Falmer in the rear, and a large bundle of orchid roots and part of their equipment filling the middle. The two Indians occupied the other boat, together with the rest of the supplies.

It was a monotonous journey. The river wound like a sluggish olive snake between dark, interminable walls of forest, from which the goblin faces of orchids leered. There were no sounds other than the splash of paddles, the furious chattering of monkeys, and petulant cries of fiery-colored birds. The sun rose above the jungle and poured down a tide of torrid brilliance.

Thone rowed steadily looking back over his shoulder at times to address Falmer with some casual remark or friendly question. The latter, with dazed eyes and features queerly pale and pinched in the sunlight, sat dully erect and made no effort to use his paddle. He offered no reply to the queries of Thone, but shook his head at intervals, with a sort of shuddering motion that was plainly involuntary. After a while he began to moan thickly, as if in pain or delirium.

They went on in this manner for hours. The heat grew more oppressive between the stifling walls of jungle. Thone became aware of a shriller cadence in the moans of his companion. Looking back, he saw that Falmer had removed his sun-helmet, seemingly oblivious of the murderous heat, and was clawing at the crown of his head with frantic fingers. Convulsions shook his entire body, the dugout began to rock dangerously as he tossed to and fro in a paroxysm of manifest agony. His voice mounted to a high un-human shrieking.

Thone made a quick decision. There was a break in the lining palisade of somber forest, and he headed the boat for shore immediately. The Indians followed, whispering between themselves and eyeing the sick man with glances of apprehensive awe and terror that puzzled Thone tremendously. He felt that there was some devilish mystery about the whole affair; and he could not imagine what was wrong with Falmer. All the known manifestations of malignant tropical diseases rose before him like a rout of hideous fantasms; but among them, he could not recognize the thing that had assailed his companion.

Having gotten Falmer ashore on a semicircle of liana-latticed beach without the aid of the Indians, who seemed unwilling to approach the sick man, Thone administered a heavy hypodermic injection of morphine from his medicine chest. This appeared to ease Falmer's suffering, and the convulsions ceased. Thone, taking advantage of their remission, proceeded to examine the crown of Falmer's head.

He was startled to find, amid the thick disheveled hair, a hard and pointed lump which resembled the tip of a beginning horn, rising under the still-unbroken skin. As if endowed with erectile and resistless life, it seemed to grow beneath his fingers.

At the same time, abruptly and mysteriously, Falmer opened his eyes and appeared to regain full consciousness; For a few minutes he was more his normal self than at any time since his return from the ruins. He began to talk, as if anxious to relieve his mind of some oppressing burden. His voice was peculiarly thick and toneless, but Thone was able to follow his mutterings and piece them together.

"The pit! The pit!," said Falmer. "The infernal thing that was in the pit, in the deep sepulcher! . . . I wouldn't go back there for the treasure of a dozen El Dorados . . . I didn't tell you much about those ruins, Thone. Somehow it was hard—impossibly hard—to talk.

"I guess the Indian knew there was something wrong with the ruins. He led me to the place . . . but he wouldn't tell me anything about it; and he waited by the riverside while I searched for the treasure.

"Great grey walls there were, older than the jungle: old as death and time. They must have been quarried and reared by people from some lost planet. They loomed and leaned at mad, unnatural angles, threatening to crush the trees about them. And there were columns, too: thick, swollen columns of unholy form, whose abominable carvings the jungle had not wholly screened from view.

"There was no trouble finding that accursed burial pit. The pavement above had broken through quite recently, I think. A big tree had pried with its boa-like roots between the flagstones that were buried beneath centuries of mold. One of the flags had been tilted back on the pavement, and another had fallen through into the pit. There was a large hole, whose bottom I could see dimly in the forest-strangled light. Something glimmered palely at the bottom; but I could not be sure what it was.

"I had taken along a coil of rope, as you remember. I tied one end of it to a main root of the tree, dropped the other through the opening, and went down like a monkey. When I got to the bottom I could see little at first in the gloom, except the whitish glimmering all around me, at my feet. Something that was unspeakably brittle and friable crunched beneath me when I began to move. I turned on my flashlight, and saw that the place was fairly littered with bones. Human skeletons lay tumbled everywhere. They must have been removed long ago . . . I groped around amid the bones and dust, feeling pretty much like a ghoul, but couldn't find anything of value, not even a bracelet or a finger-ring on any of the skeletons.

"It wasn't until I thought of climbing out that I noticed the real horror. In one of the corners—the corner nearest to the opening in the roof—I looked up and saw it in the webby shadows. Ten feet above my head it hung, and I had almost touched it, unknowingly, when I descended the rope.

"It looked like a sort of white lattice-work at first. Then I saw that the lattice was partly formed of human bones—a complete skeleton, very tall and stalwart, like that of a warrior. A pale withered thing grew out of the skull, like a set of fantastic antlers ending in myriads of long and stringy tendrils that had spread upward till they reached the roof. They must have lifted the skeleton, or body, along with them as they climbed.

"I examined the thing with my flashlight. It must have been a plant of some sort, and apparently it had started to grow in the cranium: Some of the branches had issued from the cloven crown, others through the eye holes, the mouth, and the nose holes, to flare upward. And the roots of the blasphemous thing had gone downward, trellising themselves on every bone. The very toes and fingers were ringed with them, and they drooped in writhing coils. Worst of all, the ones that had issued from the toe-ends were rooted in a second skull, which dangled just below, with fragments of the broken-off root system. There was a litter of fallen bones on the floor in the corner.

"The sight made me feel a little weak, somehow, and more than a little nauseated by that abhorrent, inexplicable mingling of the human and the plant. I started to climb the rope, in a feverish hurry to get out, but the thing fascinated me in its abominable fashion, and I couldn't help pausing to study it a little more when I had climbed halfway. I leaned toward it too fast, I guess, and the rope began to sway, bringing my face lightly against the leprous, antler-shaped boughs above the skull.

"Something broke—possibly a sort of pod on one of the branches. I found my head enveloped in a cloud of pearl-grey powder, very light, fine, and scentless. The stuff settled on my hair, it got into my nose and eyes, nearly choking and blinding me. I shook it off as well as I could. Then I climbed on and pulled myself through the opening . . ."

As if the effort of coherent narration had been too heavy a strain, Falmer lapsed into disconnected mumblings. The mysterious malady, whatever it was, returned upon him, and his delirious ramblings were mixed with groans of torture. But at moments he regained a flash of coherence.

"My head! My head!" he muttered. "There must be something in my brain, something that grows and spreads; I tell you, I can feel it there. I haven't felt right at any time since I left the burial pit . . . My mind has been queer ever since. It must have been the spores of the ancient devil-plant . . . The spores have taken root . . . The thing is splitting my skull, going down into my brain—a plant that springs out of a human cranium—as if from a flower pot!"

The dreadful convulsions began once more, and Falmer writhed uncontrollably in his companion's arms, shrieking with agony. Thone, sick at heart and shocked by his sufferings, abandoned all effort to restrain him and took up the hypodermic. With much difficulty, he managed to inject a triple dose, and Falmer grew quiet by degrees, and lay with open glassy eyes, breathing stertorously. Thone, for the first time, perceived an odd protrusion of his eyeballs, which seemed about to start from their sockets, making it impossible for the lids to close, and lending the drawn features an expression of mad horror. It was as if something were pushing Falmer's eyes from his head.

Thone, trembling with sudden weakness and terror, felt that he was involved in some unnatural web of nightmare. He could not, dared not, believe the story Falmer had told him, and its implications. Assuring himself that his companion had imagined it all, had been ill throughout with the incubation of some strange fever, he stooped over and found that the horn-shaped lump on Falmer's head had now broken through the skin.

With a sense of unreality, he stared at the object that his prying fingers had revealed amid the matted hair. It was unmistakably a plant-bud of some sort, with involuted folds of pale green and bloody pink that seemed about to expand. The thing issued from above the central suture of the skull.

A nausea swept upon Thone, and he recoiled from the lolling head and its baleful outgrowth, averting his gaze. His fever was returning, there was a woeful debility in all his limbs, and he heard the muttering voice of delirium through the quinine-induced ringing in his ears. His eyes blurred with a deathly and miasmal mist.

He fought to subdue his illness and impotence. He must not give way to it wholly; he must go on with Falmer and the Indians and reach the nearest trading station, many days away on the Orinoco, where Falmer could receive aid.

As if through sheer volition, his eyes cleared, and he felt a resurgence of strength. He looked around for the guides, and saw, with a start of uncomprehending surprise, that they had vanished. Peering further, he observed that one of the boats—the dugout used by the Indians—had also disappeared. It was plain that he and Falmer had been deserted. Perhaps the Indians had known what was wrong with the sick man, and had been afraid. At any rate, they were gone, and they had taken much of the camp equipment and most of the provisions with them.

Thone turned once more to the supine body of Falmer, conquering his repugnance with effort. Resolutely he drew out his clasp knife and, stooping over the stricken man, he excised the protruding bud, cutting as close to the scalp as he could with safety. The thing was unnaturally tough and rubbery; it exuded a thin, sanguinous fluid; and he shuddered when he saw its internal structure, full of nerve-like filaments, with a core that suggested cartilage.

He flung it aside, quickly, on the river sand. Then, lifting Falmer in his arms, he lurched and staggered towards the remaining boat. He fell more than once, and lay half swooning across the inert body. Alternately carrying and dragging his burden, he reached the boat at last. With the remainder of his failing strength, he contrived to prop Falmer in the stern against the pile of equipment.

His fever was mounting apace. After much delay, with tedious, half-delirious exertions, he pushed off from the shore, till the fever mastered him wholly and the oar slipped from oblivious fingers . . .

He awoke in the yellow glare of dawn, with his brain and his senses comparatively clear. His illness had left a great languor, but his first thought was of Falmer. He twisted about, nearly falling overboard in his debility, and sat facing his companion.

Falmer still reclined, half sitting, half lying, against the pile of blankets and other impedimenta. His knees were drawn up, his hands clasping them as if in tetanic rigor. His features had grown as stark and ghastly as those of a dead man, and his whole aspect was one of mortal rigidity. It was this, however, that caused Thone to gasp with unbelieving horror.

During the interim of Thone's delirium and his lapse into slumber, the monstrous plant bud, merely stimulated, it would seem, by the act of excision, had grown again with preternatural rapidity, from Falmer's head. A loathsome pale-green stem was mounting thickly, and had started to branch like antlers after attaining a height of six or seven inches.

More dreadful than this, if possible, similar growths had issued from the eyes; and their stems, climbing vertically across the forehead, had entirely displaced the eyeballs. Already they were branching like the thing from the crown. The antlers were all tipped with pale vermilion. They appeared to quiver with repulsive animations, nodding rhythmically in the warm, windless air . . . From the mouth another stem protruded, curling upward like a long and whitish tongue. It had not yet begun to bifurcate.

Thone closed his eyes to shut away the shocking vision. Behind his lids, in a yellow dazzle of light, he still saw the cadaverous features, the climbing stems that quivered against the dawn like ghastly hydras of tomb-etiolated green. They seemed to be waving toward him, growing and lengthening as they waved. He opened his eyes again, and fancied, with a start of new terror; that the antlers were actually taller than they had been a few moments previous.

After that, he sat watching them in a sort of baleful hypnosis. The illusion of the plant's visible growth, and freer movement—if it were illusion—increased upon him. Falmer, however, did not stir, and his parchment face appeared to shrivel and fall in, as if the roots of the growth were draining his blood, were devouring his very flesh in their insatiable and ghoulish hunger.

Thone wrenched his eyes away and stared at the river shore. The stream had widened and the current had grown more sluggish. He sought to recognize their location, looking vainly for some familiar landmark in the monotonous dull-green cliffs of jungle that lined the margin. He felt hopelessly lost and alienated. He seemed to be drifting on an unknown tide of madness and nightmare, accompanied by something more frightful than corruption itself.

His mind began to wander with an odd inconsequence, coming back always, in a sort of closed circle, to the thing that was devouring

Falmer. With a flash of scientific curiosity, he found himself wondering to what genus it belonged. It was neither fungus nor pitcher
plant, nor anything that he had ever encountered or heard of in his
explorations. It must have come, as Falmer had suggested, from an
alien world: it was nothing that the earth could conceivably have
nourished.

He felt, with a comforting assurance, that Falmer was dead. That
at least was a mercy. But even as he shaped the thought he heard a
low, guttural moaning, and, peering at Falmer in a horrible startle-
ment, saw that his limbs and body were twitching slightly. The
twitching increased, and took on a rhythmic regularity, though at
no time did it resemble the agonized and violent convulsions of the
previous day. It was plainly automatic, like a sort of galvanism; and
Thone saw that it was timed with the languorous and loathsome
swaying of the plant. The effect on the watcher was insidiously
mesmeric and somnolent; and once he caught himself beating the
detestable rhythm with his foot.

He tried to pull himself together, groping desperately for something
to which his sanity could cling. Ineluctably, his illness returned: fever,
nausea, and revulsion worse than the loathliness of death . . . But
before he yielded to it utterly, he drew his loaded revolver from the
holster and fired six times into Falmer's quivering body . . . He knew
that he had not missed, but after the final bullet Falmer still moaned
and twitched in unison with the evil swaying of the plant, and Thone,
sliding into delirium, heard still the ceaseless, automatic moaning.

There was no time in the world of seething unreality and shoreless
oblivion through which he drifted. When he came to himself again,
he could not know if hours or weeks had elapsed. But he knew at
once that the boat was no longer moving; and lifting himself dizzily,
he saw that it had floated into shallow water and mud and was nosing
the beach of a tiny, jungle-tufted isle in mid-river. The putrid odor
of slime was about him like a stagnant pool; and he heard a strident
humming of insects.

It was either late morning or early afternoon, for the sun was high
in the still heavens. Lianas were drooping above him from the island
trees like uncoiled serpents, and epiphytic orchids, marked with
ophidian mottlings, leaned toward him grotesquely from lowering
boughs. Immense butterflies went past on sumptuously spotted wings.

He sat up, feeling very giddy and lightheaded, and faced again the
horror that accompanied him. The thing had grown incredibly:
the three-antlered stems, mounting above Falmer's head, had become

gigantic and had put out masses of ropy feelers that tossed uneasily in the air, as if searching for support—or new provender. In the topmost antlers a prodigious blossom had opened—a sort of fleshy disk, broad as a man's face and white as leprosy.

Falmer's features had shrunken till the outlines of every bone were visible as if beneath tightened paper. He was a mere death's head in a mask of human skin; and beneath his clothing the body was little more than a skeleton. He was quite still now, except for the communicated quivering of the stems. The atrocious plant had sucked him dry, had eaten his vitals and his flesh.

Thone wanted to hurl himself forward in a mad impulse to grapple with the growth. But a strange paralysis held him back. The plant was like a living and sentient thing—a thing that watched him, that dominated him with its un-clean but superior will. And the huge blossom, as he stared, took on the dim, unnatural semblance of a face. It was somehow like the face of Falmer, but the lineaments were twisted all awry, and were mingled with those of something wholly devilish and nonhuman. Thone could not move—he could not take his eyes from the blasphemous abnormality.

By some miracle, his fever had left him; and it did not return. Instead, there came an eternity of frozen fright and madness in which he sat facing the mesmeric plant. It towered before him from the dry, dead shell that had been Falmer, its swollen, glutted stems and branches swaying gently, its huge flower leering perpetually upon him with its impious travesty of a human face. He thought that he heard a low, singing sound, ineffably sweet, but whether it emanated from the plant or was a mere hallucination of his overwrought senses, he could not know.

The sluggish hours went by, and a gruelling sun poured down its beams like molten lead from some titanic vessel of torture. His head swam with weakness and the fetor-laden heat, but he could not relax the rigor of his posture. There was no change in the nodding mon-strosity, which seemed to have attained its full growth above the head of its victim. But after a long interim Thone's eyes were drawn to the shrunken hands of Falmer, which still clasped the drawn-up knees in a spasmodic clutch. Through the ends of the fingers, tiny white rootlets had broken and were writhing slowly in the air, grop-ing, it seemed, for a new source of nourishment. Then from the neck and chin, other tips were breaking, and over the whole body the clothing stirred in a curious manner, as if with the crawling and lifting of hidden lizards.

At the same time the singing grew louder, sweeter, more imperious, and the swaying of the great plant assumed an indescribably seductive tempo. It was like the allurement of voluptuous sirens, the deadly languor of dancing cobras. Thone felt an irresistible compulsion: a summons was being laid upon him, and his drugged mind and body must obey it. The very fingers of Falmer, twisting viperishly, seemed beckoning to him. Suddenly he was on his hands and knees in the bottom of the boat. Inch by inch, with terror and fascination contending in his brain, he crept forward, dragging himself over the disregarded bundle of orchid-plants, inch by inch, foot by foot, till his head was against the withered hands of Falmer, from which hung and floated the questing roots.

Some cataleptic spell had made him helpless. He felt the rootlets as they moved like delving fingers through his hair and over his face and neck, and started to strike in with agonizing, needle-sharp tips. He could not stir, he could not even close his lids. In a frozen stare, he saw the gold and carmine flash of a hovering butterfly as the roots began to pierce his pupils.

Deeper and deeper went the greedy roots, while new filaments grew out to enmesh him like a witch's net . . . For a while, it seemed that the dead and the living writhed together in leashed convulsions . . . At last Thone hung supine amid the lethal, ever-growing web; bloated and colossal, the plant lived on; and in its upper branches, through the still, stifling afternoon, a second flower began to unfold.

ALONE IN SHARK WATERS

John Kruse

DOWN IN THE hold, the noise was earsplitting. Every timber, the length and breadth of the Ben Sidi Tajir, seemed to be shrieking in agony. The single hurricane lamp swung sickeningly overhead, swilling its anemic light around in the blackness. Mike Gardener shut his eyes and braced himself against a crate; he felt the ship lift and drop away crabwise in a quick, double movement that sucked his stomach about inside him like water in a goat skin.

The native passengers around him were now fully awake. They were sitting up among the cargo, chattering shrilly, the whites of their eyes showing clearly in the lamplight. There were about twenty of them, traveling freight, like himself, from Ceylon to the Maldive Islands.

The Ben Sidi Tajir was a Maldivian schooner, and her run was between Colombo and the islands. She was a cross between a felucca and a Spanish galleon, and her crew was a ragged bunch of moplas, descended from the old Malabar Coast pirates. There was nothing those moplas didn't know about the sea. They had smelled the wind coming five hours before it hit the ship. The ship was a full day out of port. There was nothing they could do but keep running and hope to miss it. When the wind was an hour away, they knew by the sky that they didn't have a chance. It was two in the morning, and Mike was asleep on deck. They had shaken him awake and told him to get below. Then they had dropped the big triangular sail, battened down the hatches and heaved to.

The only passenger accommodation was the hold, and Mike had gone down there wondering what the panic was. He didn't wonder for long. It was a hurricane.

It hit the mainmast with a shock that went right down into the ship and set up a howl in the rigging that made Mike's hackles creep. The ship was half empty, and with all her galleonlike superstructure in the stern, she began to roll like a tar barrel.

Mike braced himself with his feet and listened to the grinding timbers and cursed. There were safer ways of getting to the islands than in this relic, but not as cheap; that was the rub. When you speared fish for a living, you couldn't afford to ride fancy.

He was on his way to the Maldives to try the spearing there. He was planning to fish his way through the reefs, selling his catches as he went—a sort of working vacation. His spear gun lay on the rice sacks beside him, with his fins and mask strapped to the trigger guard. His only other baggage was a pack containing a change of clothing, a dozen harpoon heads and the sixty-foot reel he used for spearing in deep water.

The storm seemed to be getting worse. He could hear the Diesel auxiliary laboring hard in the struggle to keep the ship's head into the wind, felt the screw race in the air each time she toppled down into a trough. Near him a mopla woman lay on the sacks clutching her belly and whimpering. She was pregnant, and Mike couldn't tell if she was in labor or just seasick. She didn't seem to belong to anybody. He spoke to her in Singhalese, but she made no sign that she had heard him.

Suddenly the ship gave one of its quick, double movements. There was a slow, grinding crash, and the vessel seemed to convulse. The lantern leaped from its hook, smashed against a crate and went out. Through the infernal din Mike heard the natives screaming and, in the blackness, felt the ship heave over on its side.

His instantaneous thought was that they had hit a reef. Then he knew they couldn't have. They were a full day's sail west of Ceylon; the water here was five hundred fathoms deep. The ship was breaking up. He grabbed up his most valuable possession, the spear gun, and struggled toward the mopla woman. He fell across her and she screamed. He shouted at her that it was the American and, gripping her under the armpit, lifted her to her feet and half carried, half dragged her toward where he knew the gangway out of the hold to be.

The natives blundered together in the darkness, screaming and groping for the doorway. A match spurted near him. There was an instant of wild eyes and gleaming bodies. He spotted the gangway.

The match went out as the crowd surged forward. The next moment, he and the woman were caught up in a crazy, struggling mass. Someone grabbed onto his back, clawed a way up over him. He kept hold of the woman and his gun, and shoved.

Suddenly something gave, and they were moving forward through water already knee-deep. It was deluging down from above, and there were figures up there against a faint square of sky, trying to fight their way up through the water, but it was forcing them back. Then the boat rolled and the deluge stopped. Mike got the woman's hand and clamped it onto his belt, then heaved himself up onto the companionway. Someone got hold of his gun and tried to pull him down by it. The gun was so long that it was fouling everything, and he nearly decided to let it go. Then he changed his mind. It was his livelihood, and he had brought it all the way from Genoa.

He wrenched the gun free and struggled up the ladder. There was someone above him; he lifted him by force clean out on deck, fell on top of him, rolled over, and reached back down the hatch for the woman. He got hold of her by the hair just as a wave smashed down onto them. It flattened him against the deck; if he hadn't had hold of the woman, it would have knocked her off the ladder. Someone screamed. The water dragged at him and drained away. Mike gasped and opened his eyes.

The deck slanted right down into the sea; there were no lights anywhere. The native beside him had disappeared. He had an impression of black mountains heaving against a sulphurous sky, of smashed rigging. Another wave crashed down on him like a ton weight, but he had the woman under the arms now and her weight anchored him.

As the wave hissed away, Mike pulled her out and got her down beside him on the slanting deck. More natives stumbled up out of the hatch. He was trying to remember where the lifeboats were. But the onslaught had been so quick, the crew wouldn't have had a chance to launch them. Something was sticking into his belly. It was the gun, with the fins and mask attached to it. He picked it up and looked around for something that would float. There was a life belt against the deckhouse; he caught the gleam of it in the darkness.

He took the woman's arms and hooked them over the hatch. He waited for the ship to roll back and tried to run along the sloping deck. His plimsolls slipped. He hit the planking with a smack and began to slide.

Mike's mind cleared; beyond fear, coolly and carefully, he watched for the rail, preparing to check against it with his feet. Its silhouette stood out clearly a foot or two above the foam. Then something crashed down on top of him, and he was under water again, tons of it, black and heavy and solid. It burned up into his sinuses, filling his brain with stars. Then the weight seemed to lift, and he lifted with it, up and up and up. Then surprisingly, there was air. He gulped at it, opened his eyes, and saw the dark shape of the ship. It was below him. Scared that he would be smashed against it, he began to swim.

He swam with the wind, angling past the wreck. He was lifted and flung like a cork toward the tilted deck. A native was clinging to the rail. Mike was dashed to within a foot of him, and sucked back. He saw the shine of water on the man's back, saw him hanging in the sudden vacuum; then the sea heaved up and tore the native loose. He couldn't see what happened to him. The next moment, Mike was clear of the stern, surrounded by blackness, unable to see or to gauge the waves, trying to time his breaths to coincide with his rises to the surface. There was so much water in the air, it was difficult to tell when he was under and when he wasn't.

Hopelessness welled up in him. He was being swept away from the wreck into the raging blackness of the Indian Ocean. The nearest land was Ceylon, maybe a hundred miles to the east. He knew that no boat had got clear of the ship and that his chances of being picked up were nil. But he made no attempt to fight his way back to the vessel. If he had he would have been drowned inside of a minute, and instinctively he knew it. He kept right on with the storm, out into the vastness and the darkness. And he was afraid.

He struggled in the whirl and plunge of the waters, sobbing for air, trying to think. But he couldn't think of anything. He felt that something was dragging him under and realized that it was the spear gun. The mask and fins strapped to it were cupping the water. It was natural for him to have the gun; he didn't wonder about it any more than a carpenter would wonder about having his hammer. Its five pounds of duralumin and steel were a part of him; now they were gripped in his right hand in a clutch that nothing short of death could have broken.

The familiarity of the gun steadied him. It never occurred to him to drop it. He hugged it in to his chest and kept swimming, and a process began in the back of his mind that suddenly became defiance. He was in the sea and he had the gun. It was the same sea—the sea that was his life, the sea that he dived and hunted in every day all day—whipped up now into a frenzy, but still the same sea. There were jokes in Colombo about his being half fish. Maybe he was. Well, this was his sea.

The idea grew, and the storm seemed to change; maybe it was really letting up—he didn't know, but he knew suddenly that he could beat it, the way a fighter can sometimes tell with his opponent the first moment he comes in against him. He could ride it out, and there would be a plane. They would be bound to send out a plane.

A big wave curled over on top of him from behind and buried him in darkness. He didn't fight it; he just lay in the water holding his breath. He felt himself falling. He was out of the back of it. He breathed until he felt the lift of the next one, gasped a lungful of air, and, as it broke over him, ripped off his pants and shoes. In the next wave he got rid of his shirt. He was naked now except for his belt and knife. He thought of trying to put his fins on, but he knew he could never make it.

He needed all the buoyancy he could get. With every gasp of air, he began to swallow some. He felt the bubbles form in his stomach and fought back the desire to belch them out again.

He wrestled the spear gun around to the small of his back and clipped the butt hook onto his belt, so that he had the use of both arms.

He could lie along the surface then. It was like body-surfing, only the waves weren't breaking, they were running. Instead of carrying him with them, they swept by underneath, lifting and dropping him, with a feet-to-head movement, so far and so fast he was jarred nearly senseless. The speed of the sea against the fins and mask drove the harpoon down between his legs and turned him over. He went under and nearly didn't come up.

He didn't want to jettison the gun, so he pulled around into the wind and faced the sea. The spray was wicked, but the movement was better. The gun behind him acted as a rudder.

Mike stayed that way, with the sea tearing past him, breaking through the waves, his mind stopped down to a pin point of concentration. Keep alive, he thought. Never mind where the wind is taking you. Just keep alive. Planes will scour the whole area. Ride it. Just ride it out. You've been in a spot before. How about Iwo Jima? What did you do then? Ride it out!

Wave after wave after wave came—rush, rush, rush. The sounds dabbed and cleared in his ears monotonously, and it was the roaring and fading of sea shells, and then it was voices—loud, then soft. Then it was anesthesia, with great whirling lights and the punch-punch of watery fists in his eyes growing duller and, as time dragged by, imperceptible; he could feel nothing, and yet he knew it was still going on. There was movement and a sense of flying and sinking, but no feeling at all, nothing, and he got scared. He thought he was unconscious, that he was drowning. If only he could see something—anything—he would be able to tell!

He stared up at the sky blindly and twisted around, searching the darkness. Then behind him he saw a single, pale rent in the clouds. Dawn! Then he *was* conscious—the excitement, the relief of it. Mike twisted and began to swim toward the light but the spear gun fouled his legs instantly, and he went under.

As he sank down under the waves, something touched him. Despite his numbness, he felt it distinctly against his thigh—scaly and muscular and cold. The shock sobered him. He kicked convulsively to the surface.

The roughness and solidity had felt like a shark. He braced his muscles to resist the impact he thought must come. His softness and nakedness became huge in his mind, as they do under machine-gun fire. He sucked in his belly, beat with his legs in an effort to get up above the sea. He imagined the great shape of the shark below him negotiating the heaving water, waiting for a trough. A trough came. Mike dropped down into it, feeling his belly vulnerable and unprotected. He clenched his teeth, eyes, fists, toes, and waited. Another wave came, another trough; again the tension, again nothing. Mike knew that he would soon exhaust himself. He must relax; if it came, it came.

But it didn't come. He relaxed gradually, prayed for light and snatched another look at the east. The clouds were lifting off the horizon, revealing a long ingot of yellow light.

Hurry, hurry, he thought. But it didn't. It spread very slowly until the sea emerged from grayness and revealed itself fully, rolling and vast and lonely; he wished he had never seen it.

No creature rose to attack him, and gradually he got a hold on himself. He could handle the waves better now that he could see them; he could time his breathing. It was no worse than swimming in a monsoon sea, and he had had plenty of that.

He kept watching for a boat or a raft, but in all that endless expanse, there was only him. What of the other passengers, the crew? he wondered. Surely he wasn't the only one?

Then suddenly the wind dropped. The effect was like deafness. The wind must have been diminishing for some time, and now suddenly there wasn't a breath, only the sea whishing and washing, but no spray and no thunder against his eardrums. Relief came to him and hope, and then something more arrogant—conquest. He had outlived the wind. The loneliness was back, worse than before. The sea stretched all around, endless and inescapable.

At last, the sun itself broke the ocean's rim, blazing a trail of weaving fire across the sea. The trail elongated and merged with the sky. The waves marched on Mike now in pink-gold echelons.

He felt all beaten up. Snap out of it, he thought, remembering the shark. Soon the fish would start feeding, and killer fish got very nasty in the early morning.

He got the gun unclipped and, lying with his face in the water, unstrapped the fins and mask. He got the fins on, sinking slowly down as he fitted them onto his feet. He came up quickly, very quickly, and got the snorkel mask up out of the water and peered at it blearily. The glass was intact; so was the breathing tube. The valve which kept the water out of the tube during a dive hinged freely. Thank God, he thought. He emptied the mask out, spat on the glass to stop it from clouding when he breathed, rinsed the mask out again, pulled it on and took a quick look down into the water. He did not know why he was so jumpy; there was nothing down there—only a few small shapes in the grayness. There wasn't enough light yet to see deep.

The harpoon was lashed against the barrel of the spear gun with the steel line. Lying on his face again but breathing now through the snorkel tube—interruptedly, because the high sea kept dabbing the valve shut—Mike unwound the line and got the harpoon into the projector. He wrestled with the propulsion unit for nearly a minute before he managed to compress the heavy, double spring. As he floated to the surface and lay there, gasping weakly, he knew that that was the last time he would have the strength to do that. One shot—that was all he had.

The undersea dawned slowly beneath him. The rising sun rayed down through the plankton particles in bewildering, shifting patterns. He saw numerous fish, all fairly well down and shadowy still. It looked unbelievably deep. Something seemed to open up in his diaphragm and let the draught in. There would be fish out here he didn't know about—predatory giants as different from their reef relations as lions from alley cats.

The farther the sun got down into the water, the more fish he could see. Five, six, seven fathoms—there were fish and more fish, the deepest gleaming in the blue-blackness like sunken coins. Even as he watched, the pulse of their actions seemed to quicken. A pack of big bluefish cut into a shoal of mackerel four fathoms below him. The mackerel raced off in a tight, terrified wedge. It had started.

The whole of the visible undersea seemed to speed up like a film. The fish became no more than streaks of color in the ice-blue upper fathoms, tracing firework patterns of fear and hunger. Jacks and bonitos were everywhere, sometimes combining to tear with snapping jaws into a big shoal, then turning on one another to fight for the spoils.

The water became filled with little puffs of blood. The smell of it seemed to excite the fish to even greater ferocity and fear. This battle period lasted, normally, half an hour in the morning and the same again at nightfall. Mike wished to hell they would stop. Barracuda and sharks went crazy at feeding time; they seemed to lose all their normal fear of noise and hostile action and behaved much more in accordance with their reputation.

Suddenly three six-foot torpedolike shapes shot up out of the depths toward him. He had barely time to pull himself together before they had veered off and beaten away into the blueness. They were gun metal and silver, and shaped like gigantic mackerel—tuna. Hell, he was slow! He realized then what a sitting target he was. Lucky that was all they had been; his reflexes were all to pieces from the storm.

Almost at once another big shape appeared below him, followed by several more. They moved through the water with a sickening rush, the big one in front working its jaws like a buzz saw. They were blue shark, with pectorals like bomb fins, and paper-knife noses. Mike didn't have time to stir a muscle. They swept by underneath him, the big one spitting out fragments of fish into the water, which were snapped up by the ones behind. They were gone in an instant, and he was just letting go his breath when suddenly they were back.

It was as evil a procession as one could ever wish not to see: three pilot fish were above and slightly in front, their stripes fairly screaming danger; behind them came a ten-foot chunk of barrel-like blue muscle and, bringing up the rear, four half-grown versions of the same creature.

The sharks surged by, slamming their jaws, and disappeared into the dimness. Mike lay in the water and waited; but this time they didn't come back.

He sucked in a deep breath. It had been a matron shark airing the kids. If a plane didn't hurry up and come soon, he thought . . .

Presently, the tempo of the underwater slowed down. Breakfast was over. Mike relaxed, flattened on the surface, beating automatically with his fins, rising and falling steadily, saving his strength. The sun climbed slowly up the sky. He was really tired now, tired and thirsty. He estimated that he had been in the water for seven hours. During a full day's spearing he sometimes kept going for eight without touching down. But that was in a calm sea and in sight of land. Land, he thought longingly, with the elephants plowing the coconut groves along by the sea.

It must have been about eleven o'clock when he heard the plane. He hoisted himself as far up in the water as he could and ripped off his mask. He saw it at once. It was a biplane. It was puttering over the sea about a mile to the north, with its nose high, obviously on the lookout for something. Mike waved his mask frantically, shouted and splashed about in the water, but it kept going steadily, and eventually disappeared over the horizon.

It'll be back, he thought wildly. It's looking for the wreck. It's got to come back! He kept the mask off, forgetting the danger, forgetting everything but that up there was a fellow human being and that he must make him see him. His heart began to thump, and a great deadness spread outward from his diaphragm into his limbs.

The waves lifted and dropped him. From the crest of each he craned toward the horizon, openmouthed, hoping to hear the engine. An especially big wave heaved up in front of him. He glanced at it, gauging it automatically, then stared at it, shocked. Incased in it, as though in green ice, was a shark. It was drifting sideways in the wave, its dorsal fin lazily breaking the crest.

In a moment it would be on top of him. He threshed about with his fins to scare it, at the same time fumbling with the mask. He got it on—half filled with water—blew it out and dived.

The creature had gone. He twisted around under the water. It was behind him. It was a heavily mottled shark, seven or eight feet long. It had seen him, all right, and seemed idly curious. With a careless flick of its big tail, it nosed to within six feet of him.

Mike had one idea in mind; that was to get rid of it. Spreading his arms and legs, he hooted into the mask.

The shark's languor left it instantly. With a bewilderingly swift movement, it turned and shot away at right angles; stopped, turned and hung there, staring at Mike with its little, catlike eyes.

* * *

He cursed. These pelagic sharks weren't like the reef ones. That would have been enough even for a blackfin. He raised one ear out of the water and listened for the plane. It was coming! Its clatter reached him clearly over the waves. He took another look at the shark. Did he dare ignore it? The shark made a movement.

God! Mike thought. Not now. It can't come at me now!

But that was just what it did. He had to face it. He headed straight for it; desperation lent him strength.

Uncertainly the shark checked its advance with its pectorals. Mike kept right on, and when he was a dozen feet away from the shark he blew a burst of bubbles at it through his snorkel tube. The big mottled body jackknifed and turned and fled, thudding the water with its tail.

Mike hit the surface and snatched off the mask all in one move-ment. The roar of the plane spanked his ears like a thunderclap. It was right overhead. He tried to shout, but he hadn't any air. He gasped to fill his lungs, took in some water, and choked.

The blind belly of the plane passed over him. It was an old Gladiator, with fixed undercarriage. He managed to get the gun up and wagged the duralumin in the sunlight, but the plane just pulled away steadily across the waves. He made a noise at last, something between a gasp and a scream. It just had to see him! Weird sounds dragged from his throat as he watched the machine diminish, and heard the engine grow fainter, fainter, then merge with the rush of the sea.

He was alone. He subsided, exhausted, into the waves, lying there weak and uncaring, letting the water drain into his parted mouth, letting its green weight close over him.

Oh, God, he thought. Oh, God, oh, God, oh, God.

The sun had swung over behind him and was sinking slowly toward the sea. He had been swimming since morning, weakly but steadily. After the plane, he had lain in the water a while; then some inward strength had got hold of him, turned him toward the eastern horizon, and forced his limbs to move.

Everything that was reasonable in him resisted. If another plane or a ship were to come, it would come; swimming wouldn't help. And if it didn't come the sharks would. Land, allowing the maximum for drift, was about seventy miles away, and he had never swum more than twenty in his life.

But the stubborn spirit in him did not listen. It only knew that there was land over there below the eastern rim, solid and sweet-smelling and green, and that here there was only death. It drew him through the water—desperately.

His thighs were cramping a little, and he had chafe from the fins across the insteps of both feet. When they began to bleed, the sharks would pick up his trail, and yet he kept on, at intervals rolling his head up—sideways, to save energy—to look along the sea and at the sky. They were clear and empty and endless, and the light was glorious. He felt small in so much emptiness.

From his mouth and his throat right down to his stomach, he was puckered dry with brine. There wasn't a bead of moisture left in him. He wouldn't last the day. Sea creatures like Halloween masks came and went, appearing suddenly an inch from his face, then darting away. All day it had been the same, and he had let them come, grateful for their company.

Now suddenly he shortened the gun in his hand, jabbed at one with the protruding spear and transfixed it. He trapped its fin movements with his fingers, glancing round instinctively. Experience had taught him that often when you speared a fish, sharks, drawn by the sound of finny panic in the water, jumped you so fast they might have been fired at you.

He waited. Nothing happened. Without any conscious reasoning, Mike turned on his back and wrenched the fish off the barb, pushed back the mask and squeezed the lymphatic juices from its wound into his mouth. They were rank and oily and mingled with blood, but they were free from salt, and he wondered vaguely how he had known they would be.

When he had squeezed the fish dry, he threw it as far from him as possible and spiked another. He caught six; then, using his knife, cut the last one, a sea bream, into strips and ate it raw.

He felt strange and defiant, and when he sprawled back under the water, he felt no nausea but a sort of amazement. He would get stronger; he could keep alive for days like this. Then reason reasserted itself. Not without sleep, it said. His eyelids felt heavy at the thought of it. His legs stopped beating. The water was soft and warm. The movement of the waves had subsided to a soothing rhythm. His head sank.

Suddenly his eyes flicked open, and he was staring along the under-glow of his own stomach. A yard from his legs was the bluish head of a shark.

He slapped the water with both fins and got himself around some-how. The solid body flicked sideways and circled lazily around him. It was more than twice his length. Then somehow there was another, rock-steady in the water and growing toward him. Mike knew he couldn't fight them. He hadn't the strength. They circled around him, puzzled by his reluctance to escape.

Mike watched them, heavy-eyed; watched a third one come—smaller, this one, with a newtlike head and dappled like a newt—a tiger shark.

There was always the gun. It was his ace, he thought, admitting to himself now what had been in the back of his mind all along. He would put it under his chin and squeeze the trigger with his bare heels.

Now, he thought. Before it's too late. The deliberate circles were narrowing steadily. He lay in the water wondering vaguely why he didn't act. There seemed to be five of them now, then six.

The undersea was darkening fast. Feeding time, he thought. They would go crazy, and it would be too late to do anything. But still he lay in the water. Deep down in him there was something that refused to die. Coward! he said angrily.

Then he was panning the gun carefully, aiming at the tiger, cen-tering on one eye. And he knew why: it was half-grown and softer-skinned than the others, and he had to cripple it. It came in close. At seven feet he let the shark have it.

There was the sound of slithering steel and a blur and a jolt. The gun leaped out of his hand, and he was gasping air through the snorkel while the shark spun around in a tight clockwise circle. It didn't pull out of it or stop, but just tore on round and round like a Catherine wheel, and Mike knew he'd got it right in the eye.

The other sharks froze in the water; surprised, they hung there for a full moment; then they got it. All five of them hit the tiger together, rending and snapping crazily. A great cloud of blood spread in the water.

Mike dragged himself away from the scene. It was better without the gun. He swam until he couldn't go another stroke. Then he lay out in the water, panting so hard that the mask sucked in against his face with every breath.

He stared back behind him, but there was only a redness. Nothing came after him. He had played his ace.

There was no moon. The water heaved in the sultry darkness, glim-mering with phosphorescence. Stars drifted above and below him. He seemed to be beating slowly through space. Darkness engulfed him; then schizopod shrimps would rise like lonely suns, thicken into constellations and drift away, and brilliant dusts would form on the undertide, then condense and flood the sea with protozoic flame. He watched his hands, leprous and white, grope through the fiery sea and traced with half-dreaming eyes the comet paths of fish. Then there was only darkness, blacker than before.

He would lift his head with an effort, into the cooler air, check with the dimmer stars for east, and hear the immeasurable sigh of the ocean. Sometimes he heard across the waves, like a gun, the sound of manta hitting the sea, and knew that somewhere nearby great thirty-foot bodies were rushing together, leaping high into the air, pressed wing tip to wing tip in their mating dance.

The Pleiades swung, and the waters gleamed and died, and once something vast and terrible rose like a city in the waves. Mike heard the water draining from its sides and saw its darkness blotting out the sea. It made a sound—something between a hiss and a moan—and presently it slid back into the depths. He heard the water sucking down after it long after it had gone.

Another sun rose, a burning eye set level with the sea. And still Mike's legs were moving, just moving. Now, he thought, now the sharks will come again, and he thought of them as only liberators who would free him from the instinct that tortured him on.

Again the undersea dawn began, and nothing came—nothing but jellies, colored like sunset on ice, filling the sea with their tilted, opening-and-closing parasols; and the dorados, they came. With a glint of gold and greeny-blue, they skidded into him and turned him over. They were under him and over him and around him and away, kicking up the water in bursts of saline fire. And there was blood in the sea where the tuna caught the dorados. And still nothing came.

Mike caught a fish in his hands and ate it. He couldn't see any sense in it, but he couldn't stop himself either. His legs continued to move, almost automatically, and at high noon he saw his mother, her little-girl face collapsed with age, and she was saying in her child-voice: "All failure is a kind of death," and he thought how right she was. He had forgotten her failure with the old man. It seemed to him then that they were still together and perfectly happy. He was a little crazy.

And then a shark came. It came up behind him in the molten-metal sea, cutting through the water like the keel of a sailing ship.

Come on, you dog, Mike said to it, and: You're late! Just like the ten-o'clock scholar. (He was back at school.)

He waited for it, but it wouldn't come in, just sniffed at his fins and took a wide turn around him. He wanted it to come in, but it wouldn't take him. Yesterday he had wanted to live, but now he didn't care. If he could have slept, he would have been all right, but now he just wanted the shark to hurry up and get it over with.

So he turned his back, and when he looked round again the shark was gone. It stayed gone, and the sun burned down on the sea, which became like watered silk, very glossy and silent, and the sound he made blowing through the snorkel seemed to grow very loud, like the roaring of the locomotives in Bay St. Louis station. He relaxed into a kind of dream, and he was back in the old city, in the old apartment, dirty from working at the garage. The old man was there, and Mike had just said he couldn't stick it any more with Mum gone and everything shot to pieces the way it was—that he was heading for the Far East, Ceylon maybe. His old man looked up at him over the tops of his glasses, with his mouth turned down and his eyes preoccupied with other people and other places, and, seeing him like that, Mike suddenly realized that he really was an old man.

Then the sun drowned in a sea of blood, and he was alone in the dusk with night moving up the sky. This was his last night, he thought. Tonight he would die. There was nothing left in him to regret with or to pray with, nothing but this instinct driving him on with limbs he could no longer feel.

At last the sharks came. They came with the departing light, like slim blades in the sea. There was nothing to stop them, but they came on carefully, avoiding his fire-trail in the darkening water. He closed his eyes. It was getting late.

The sunset's imprisoned image burned dimly in his brain, like a candle guttering low, and sounds grew enormous in the water. For an instant, poised on the edge of delirium, he heard the whisper of his own fins and, behind them, the shudder of tails, like someone thrumming the deadened bass string of a harp with their fingernails. The tempo increased. Now, he thought. At last! The water shook against him, beat on his eardrums, diminished and was still.

His lids flickered. Below, in the iridescence, fish-trails sparkled through the water like a million shooting stars. They streaked ahead of him and were gone; then more, in gleaming panic, raced by—then more and more.

There was thunder in the sea, but he didn't hear it. He fell into a dreamy state. It seemed to him that the waters were boiling around him with phosphorescent light; that he was lifted and flung, buffeted by tails, flung again; that in the luminosity he saw the ocean packed solid with gleaming backs, heard their panting and heaving. Then he was down under the water, and the migrating false killer whales were above him, lighted by the phosphorescence, belly upon belly, rank upon rank.

Then somehow there was air and the sea eddied and gleamed, and the turmoil rumbled away across the sea, and he was alone.

A light forced its way under his lids, and he turned away from it. There were cold bodies around him, and when he moved they squirmed. It was still a dream, and it was wrong somehow that there should be a man in it, holding a lamp, and, in the dimness, others staring at him.

They wore ragged sarongs, and they looked for all the world like Singhalese fishermen. For some reason their eyes were wide and frightened. Their hands were dragging at a net; Mike realized suddenly that he was in the net—caught!

He learned later that he had wound up a mile off Galle, South Ceylon. He never knew how; probably the current had been working with him all the way. But somehow he had made it. The fishermen admitted afterward that they had thought he was some strange kind of monster and had nearly lit into him with their gaffs. The incident certainly gave rise to some queer tales which Mike didn't altogether like. The Ceylon Courier gave him a full-page spread. "Fish-man," the article called him again and again, and when he got out of the hospital and went down into Colombo, people looked at him strangely and weren't quite sure what to do with their eyes when they talked to him. He never spoke about it much himself, because of the feeling he had had in the net.

He knew it was a net and that they were men around him—and he was afraid. The lamp seemed to draw his eyes till the flame filled his mind, and in the darkness all around, there was terror. He gasped for air, but none would come. He struggled, and the other fish around him struggled, and he twisted and kicked, knowing only that he must get back to the sea, that he must slither back somehow into the dark cavern of the water and dart away through the softness and the silence to where he belonged. It was a sensation of the purest fear—uninhibited by logic or pride or anything human, undiluted and nightmarish—such as only a wild creature might feel when it falls a victim to man.

Then one of the natives bent over him and took off his fouled-up mask, and there was air in a cool rush and he blacked out.

THE MAN WHO WOULD BE KING

Rudyard Kipling

"Brother to a Prince and fellow to a beggar if he be found worthy."

THE LAW, AS quoted, lays down a fair conduct of life, and one not easy to follow. I have been fellow to a beggar again and again under circumstance which prevented either of us finding out whether the other was worthy. I have still to be brother to a Prince, though I once came near to kinship with what might have been a veritable King and was promised the reversion of a Kingdom—army, law-courts, revenue and policy all complete. But, to-day, I greatly fear that my King is dead, and if I want a crown I must go and hunt it for myself.

The beginning of everything was in a railway train upon the road to Mhow from Ajmir. There had been a Deficit in the Budget, which necessitated traveling, not Second-class, which is only half as dear as First-class, but by Intermediate, which is very awful indeed. There are no cushions in the Intermediate class, and the population are either Intermediate, which is Eurasian, or native, which for a long night journey is nasty, or Loafer, which is amusing though intoxicated. Intermediates do not patronize refreshment-rooms. They carry their food in bundles and pots, and buy sweets from the native sweetmeat sellers, and drink the roadside water. That is why in the hot weather Intermediates are taken out of the carriages dead, and in all weathers are most properly looked down upon.

My particular Intermediate happened to be empty till I reached Nasirabad, when a huge gentleman in shirt-sleeves entered, and, following the custom of Intermediates, passed the time of day. He was a wanderer and a vagabond like myself, but with an educated taste for whisky. He told tales of things he had seen and done, of out-of-the-way corners of the Empire into which he had penetrated, and of adventures in which he risked his life for a few days' food. "If India was filled with men like you and me, not knowing more than the crows where they'd get their next day's rations, it isn't seventy millions of revenue the land would be paying—it's seven hundred millions," said he; and as I looked at his mouth and chin I was disposed to agree with him. We talked politics—the politics of Loaferdom that sees things from the underside where the lath and plaster is not smoothed off—and we talked postal arrangements because my friend wanted to send a telegram back from the next station to Ajmir, which is the turning-off place from the Bombay to the Mhow line as you travel westward. My friend had no money beyond eight annas which he wanted for dinner, and I had no money at all, owing to the hitch in the Budget before mentioned. Further, I was going into a wilderness where, though I should resume touch with the Treasury, there were no telegraph offices. I was, therefore, unable to help him in any way.

"We might threaten a Station-master, and make him send a wire on tick," said my friend, "but that'd mean inquiries for you and for me, and I've got my hands full these days. Did you say you were traveling back along this line within any days?"

"Within ten," I said.

"Can't you make it eight?" said he. "Mine is rather urgent business."

"I can send your telegram within ten days if that will serve you," I said.

"I couldn't trust the wire to fetch him now I think of it. It's this way. He leaves Delhi on the 23d for Bombay. That means he'll be running through Ajmir about the night of the 23d."

"But I'm going into the Indian Desert," I explained.

"Well *and* good," said he. "You'll be changing at Marwar Junction to get into Jodhpore territory—you must do that—and he'll be coming through Marwar Junction in the early morning of the 24th by the Bombay Mail. Can you be at Marwar Junction on that time? 'Twon't be inconveniencing you, because I know that there's precious few pickings to be got out of those Central India States—even though you pretend to be correspondent of the *Backwoodsman*."

"Have you ever tried that trick?" I asked.

"Again and again, but the Residents find you out, and then you get escorted to the Border before you've time to get your knife into them. But about my friend here. I *must* give him word o' mouth to tell him what's come to me or else he won't know where to go. I would take it more than kind of you if you was to come out of Central India in time to catch him at Marwar Junction, and say to him: 'He has gone South for the week.' He'll know what that means. He's a big man with a red beard, and a great swell he is. You'll find him sleeping like a gentleman with all his luggage round him in a Second-class compartment. But don't you be afraid. Slip down the window and say: 'He has gone South for the week,' and he'll tumble. It's only cutting your time of stay in those parts by two days. I ask you as a stranger—going to the West," he said with emphasis.

"Where have *you* come from?" said I.

"From the East," said he, "and I am hoping that you will give him the message on the square—for the sake of my Mother as well as your own."

Englishmen are not usually softened by appeals to the memory of their mothers, but for certain reasons, which will be fully apparent, I saw fit to agree.

"It's more than a little matter," said he, "and that's why I ask you to do it—and now I know that I can depend on you doing it. A Second-class carriage at Marwar Junction, and a red-haired man asleep in it. You'll be sure to remember. I get out at the next station, and I must hold on there till he comes or sends me what I want."

"I'll give the message if I catch him," I said, "and for the sake of your Mother as well as mine I'll give you a word of advice. Don't try to run the Central India States just now as the correspondent of the *Backwoodsman*. There's a real one knocking about here, and it might lead to trouble."

"Thank you," said he simply, "and when will the swine be gone? I can't starve because he's ruining my work. I wanted to get hold of the Degumber Rajah down here about his father's widow, and give him a jump."

"What did he do to his father's widow, then?"

"Filled her up with red pepper and slippered her to death as she hung from a beam. I found that out myself and I'm the only man that would dare going into the State to get hush-money for it. They'll try to poison me, same as they did in Chortumna when I went on the loot there. But you'll give the man at Marwar Junction my message?"

He got out at a little roadside station, and I reflected. I had heard, more than once, of men personating correspondents of newspapers and bleeding small Native States with threats of exposure, but I had never met any of the caste before. They lead a hard life, and generally die with great suddenness. The Native States have a wholesome horror of English newspapers, which may throw light on their peculiar methods of government, and do their best to choke correspondents with champagne, or drive them out of their mind with four-in-hand barouches. They do not understand that nobody cares a straw for the internal administration of Native States so long as oppression and crime are kept within decent limits, and the ruler is not drugged, drunk or diseased from one end of the year to the other. Native States were created by Providence in order to supply picturesque scenery, tigers and tall writing. They are the dark places of the earth, full of unimaginable cruelty, touching the Railway and the Telegraph on one side, and on the other the days of Harun-al-Raschid. When I left the train I did business with divers Kings, and in eight days passed through many changes of life. Sometimes I wore dress clothes and consorted with Princes and Politicals, drinking from crystal and eating from silver. Sometimes I lay out upon the ground and devoured what I could get from a plate made of a flapjack, and drank the running water, and slept under the same rug as my servant. It was all in the day's work.

Then I headed for the Great Indian Desert upon the proper date, as I had promised, and the night Mail set me down at Marwar Junction, where a funny little happy-go-lucky, native-managed railway runs to Jodhpore. The Bombay Mail from Delhi makes a short halt at Marwar. She arrived as I got in, and I had just time to hurry to her platform and go down the carriages. There was only one Second-class on the train. I slipped the window and looked down upon a flaming red beard, half-covered by a railway rug. That was my man, fast asleep, and I dug him gently in the ribs. He woke with a grunt and I saw his face in the light of the lamps. It was a great and shining face.

"Tickets again?" said he.

"No," said I. "I am to tell you that he is gone South for the week. He is gone South for the week!"

The train had begun to move out. The red man rubbed his eyes. "He has gone South for the week," he repeated. "Now that's just like his impidence. Did he say that I was to give you anything? 'Cause I won't."

"He didn't," I said and dropped away, and watched the red lights die out in the dark. It was horribly cold because the wind was blowing off the sands. I climbed into my own train—not an Intermediate Carriage this time—and went to sleep.

If the man with the beard had given me a rupee I should have kept it as a memento of a rather curious affair. But the consciousness of having done my duty was my only reward.

Later on I reflected that two gentlemen like my friends could not do any good if they foregathered and personated correspondents of newspapers, and might, if they "stuck up" one of the little rat-trap States of Central India or Southern Rajputana, get themselves into serious difficulties. I therefore took some trouble to describe them as accurately as I could remember to people who would be interested in deporting them: and succeeded, so I was later informed, in having them headed back from the Degumber borders.

Then I became respectable, and returned to an Office where there were no Kings and no incidents except the daily manufacture of a newspaper. A newspaper office seems to attract every conceivable sort of person to the prejudice of discipline. Zenana-mission ladies arrive, and beg that the Editor will instantly abandon all his duties to describe a Christian prize-giving in a back slum of a perfectly inaccessible village; Colonels who have been overpassed for commands sit down and sketch the outline of a series of ten, twelve or twenty-four leading articles on Seniority *versus* Selection; missionaries wish to know why they have not been permitted to escape from their regular vehicles of abuse and swear at a brother missionary under special patronage of the editorial We; stranded theatrical companies troop up to explain that they cannot pay for their advertisements, but on their return from New Zealand or Tahiti will do so with interest; inventors of patent punkah-pulling machines, carriage couplings and unbreakable swords and axletrees call with specifications in their pockets and hours at their disposal; tea companies enter and elaborate their prospectuses with the office pens; secretaries of ball committees clamor to have the glories of their last dance more fully expounded; strange ladies rustle in and say: "I want a hundred lady's cards printed *at once,* please," which is manifestly part of an editor's duty; and every dissolute ruffian that ever tramped the Grand Trunk Road makes it his business to ask for employment as a proofreader. And, all the time, the telephone bell is ringing madly, and Kings are being killed on the Continent, and Empires are saying: "You're another," and Mister Gladstone is calling down brimstone upon the British Dominions, and the little black copy boys are whining *"kaa-pi chay-ha-yeh"* (copy wanted) like tired bees, and most of the paper is as blank as Modred's shield.

But that is the amusing part of the year. There are other six months wherein none ever come to call, and the thermometer walks inch by inch up to the top of the glass, and the office is darkened to just above reading light, and the press machines are red-hot of touch, and nobody writes anything but accounts of amusements in the Hill-stations, or obituary notices. Then the telephone becomes a tinkling terror, because it tells you of the sudden deaths of men and women that you knew intimately, and the prickly heat covers you as with a garment, and you sit down and write: "A slight increase of sickness is reported from the Khuda Janta Khan District. The outbreak is purely sporadic in its nature, and thanks to the energetic efforts of the District authorities, is now almost at an end. It is, however, with deep regret we record the death, etc."

Then the sickness really breaks out, and the less recording and reporting the better for the peace of the subscribers. But the Empires and Kings continue to divert themselves as selfishly as before, and the Foreman thinks that a daily paper really ought to come out once in twenty-four hours, and all the people at the Hill-stations in the middle of their amusements say: "Good gracious! Why can't the paper be sparkling? I'm sure there's plenty going on up here."

That is the dark half of the moon, and as the advertisements say, "must be experienced to be appreciated."

It was in that season, and a remarkably evil season, that the paper began running the last issue of the week on Saturday night, which is to say Sunday morning, after the custom of a London paper. This was a great convenience, for immediately after the paper was put to bed the dawn would lower the thermometer from 96° to almost 84° for half an hour, and in that chill—you have no idea how cold is 84° on the grass until you begin to pray for it—a very tired man could set off to sleep ere the heat roused him.

One Saturday night it was my pleasant duty to put the paper to bed alone. A King or courtier or a courtesan or a community was going to die or get a new constitution, or do something that was important on the other side of the world, and the paper was to be held open till the latest possible minute in order to catch the telegram. It was a pitchy black night, as stifling as a June night can be, and the *loo*, the red-hot wind from the westward, was booming among the tinder-dry trees and pretending that the rain was on its heels. Now and again a spot of almost boiling water would fall on the dust with the flop of a frog, but all our weary world knew that was only pretence. It was a shade cooler in the press-room than the office, so I sat there while the type clicked and clicked, and the night-jars hooted at the windows, and the all but naked compositors wiped the sweat from their foreheads and called for water. The thing that was keeping us back, whatever it was, would not come off, though the *loo* dropped and the last type was set, and the whole round earth stood still in the choking heat, with its finger on its lip, to wait the event. I drowsed, and wondered whether the telegraph was a blessing, and whether this dying man or struggling people was aware of the inconvenience the delay was causing. There was no special reason beyond the heat and worry to make tension, but as the clock hands crept up to three o'clock and the machines spun their flywheels two and three times to see that all was in order, before I said the word that would set them off, I could have shrieked aloud.

Then the roar and rattle of the wheels shivered the quiet into little bits. I rose to go away, but two men in white clothes stood in front of me. The first one said: "It's him!" The second said: "So it is!" And they both laughed almost as loudly as the machinery roared, and mopped their foreheads. "We see there was a light burning across the road and we were sleeping in that ditch there for cool-ness, and I said to my friend here: 'The office is open. Let's come along and speak to him as turned us back from the Degumber State,'" said the smaller of the two. He was the man I had met in the Mhow train, and his fellow was the red-bearded man of Marwar Junction. There was no mistaking the eyebrows of the one or the beard of the other.

I was not pleased, because I wished to go to sleep, not to squabble with loafers. "What do you want?" I asked.

"Half an hour's talk with you cool and comfortable, in the office," said the red-bearded man. "We'd *like* some drink—the Contrack doesn't begin yet, Peachey, so you needn't look—but what we really want is advice. We don't want money. We ask you as a favor, because you did us a bad turn about Degumber."

I led from the press-room to the stifling office with the maps on the walls, and the red-haired man rubbed his hands. "That's something like," said he. "This was the proper shop to come to. Now, sir, let me introduce to you Brother Peachey Carnehan, that's him, and Brother Daniel Dravot, that is *me,* and the less said about our pro-fessions the better, for we have been most things in our time. Soldier, sailor, compositor, photographer, proofreader, street preacher, and correspondents of the *Backwoodsman* when we thought the paper wanted one. Carnehan is sober, and so am I. Look at us first and see that's sure. It will save you cutting into my talk. We'll take one of your cigars apiece, and you shall see us light."

I watched the test. The men were absolutely sober, so I gave them each a tepid peg.

"Well *and* good," said Carnehan of the eyebrows, wiping the froth from his mustache. "Let me talk now, Dan. We have been all over India, mostly on foot. We have been boiler-fitters, engine-drivers, petty contractors, and all that, and we have decided that India isn't big enough for such as us."

They certainly were too big for the office. Dravot's beard seemed to fill half the room and Carnehan's shoulders the other half, as they sat on the big table. Carnehan continued: "The country isn't half worked out because they that governs it won't let you touch it. They spend all their blessed time in governing it, and you can't lift a spade, nor chip a rock, nor look for oil, nor anything like that without all the Government saying: 'Leave it alone and let us govern.' Therefore, such as it is, we will let it alone, and go away to some other place where a man isn't crowded and can come to his own. We are not little men, and there is nothing that we are afraid of except Drink, and we have signed a Contrack on that. *Therefore* we are going away to be Kings."

"Kings in our own right," muttered Dravot.

"Yes, of course," I said. "You've been tramping in the sun, and it's a very warm night, and hadn't you better sleep over the notion? Come to-morrow."

"Neither drunk nor sunstruck," said Dravot. "We have slept over the notion half a year, and require to see Books and Atlases, and we have decided that there is only one place now in the world that two strong men can Sar-a-*whack*. They call it Kafiristan. By my reckoning it's the top right-hand corner of Afghanistan, not more than three hundred miles from Peshawar. They have two-and-thirty heathen idols there, and we'll be the thirty-third. It's a mountainous country, and the women of those parts are very beautiful."

"But that is provided against in the Contrack," said Carnehan. "Neither Women nor Liquor, Daniel."

"And that's all we know, except that no one has gone there, and they fight, and in any place where they fight a man who knows how to drill men can always be a King. We shall go to those parts and say to any King we find: 'D'you want to vanquish your foes?' and we will show him how to drill men; for that we know better than anything else. Then we will subvert that King and seize his Throne and establish a Dy-nasty."

"You'll be cut to pieces before you're fifty miles across the Border," I said. "You have to travel through Afghanistan to get to that country.

It's one mass of mountains and peaks and glaciers, and no Englishman has been through it. The people are utter brutes, and even if you reached them you couldn't do anything."

"That's more like," said Carnehan. "If you could think us a little more mad we would be more pleased. We have come to you to know about this country, to read a book about it, and to be shown maps. We want you to tell us that we are fools and to show us your books." He turned to the bookcases.

"Are you at all in earnest?" I said.

"A little," said Dravot sweetly. "As big a map as you have got, even if it's all blank where Kafiristan is, and any books you've got. We can read, though we aren't very educated."

I uncased the big thirty-two-miles-to-the-inch map of India, and two smaller Frontier maps, hauled down volume INF-KAN of the *Encyclopædia Brittanica,* and the men consulted them.

"See here!" said Dravot, his thumb on the map. "Up to Jagdallak, Peachey and me know the road. We was there with Roberts' Army. We'll have to turn off to the right at Jagdallak through Laghmann territory. Then we get among the hills—fourteen thousand feet— fifteen thousand—it will be cold work there, but it don't look very far on the map."

I handed him Wood on the *Sources of the Oxus.* Carnehan was deep in the *Encyclopædia.*

"They're a mixed lot," said Dravot reflectively; "and it won't help us to know the names of their tribes. The more tribes the more they'll fight, and the better for us. From Jagdallak to Ashang. H'mm!"

"But all the information about the country is as sketchy and inac- curate as can be," I protested. "No one knows anything about it really. Here's the file of the *United Services' Institute.* Read what Bellew says."

"Blow Bellew!" said Carnehan. "Dan, they're an all-fired lot of heathens, but this book here says they think they're related to us English."

I smoked while the men pored over *Raverty, Wood,* the maps and the *Encyclopædia.*

"There is no use your waiting," said Dravot politely. "It's about four o'clock now. We'll go before six o'clock if you want to sleep, and we won't steal any of the papers. Don't you sit up. We're two harmless lunatics, and if you come to-morrow evening down to the Serai we'll say good-by to you."

"You *are* two fools," I answered. "You'll be turned back at the Frontier or cut up the minute you set foot in Afghanistan. Do you want any money or a recommendation down-country? I can help you to the chance of work next week."

"Next week we shall be hard at work ourselves thank you," said Dravot. "It isn't so easy being a King as it looks. When we've got our Kingdom in going order we'll let you know, and you can come up and help us to govern it."

"Would two lunatics make a Contrack like that?" said Carnehan, with subdued pride, showing me a greasy half-sheet of note-paper on which was written the following. I copied it, then and there, as a curiosity:

This Contract between me and you persuing witnesseth in the name of God—Amen and so forth.

(One)	That me and you will settle this matter together: *i.e.,* to be Kings of Kafiristan.
(Two)	That you and me will not, while this matter is being settled, look at any Liquor, nor any Woman black, white or brown, so as to get mixed up with one or the other harmful.
(Three)	That we conduct ourselves with dignity and discretion, and if one of us gets into trouble the other will stay by him.

Signed by you and me this day.
Peachey Taliaferro Carnehan.
Daniel Dravot.
Both Gentlemen at Large.

"There was no need for the last article," said Carnehan, blushing modestly; "but it looks regular. Now you know the sort of men that loafers are—we *are* loafers, Dan, until we get out of India—and *do* you think that we would sign a Contrack like that unless we was in earnest? We have kept away from the two things that make life worth having."

"You won't enjoy your lives much longer if you are going to try this idiotic adventure. Don't set the office on fire," I said, "and go away before nine o'clock."

I left them still poring over the maps and making notes on the back of the "Contrack." "Be sure to come down to the Serai to-morrow," were their parting words.

The Kumharsen Serai is the great foursquare sink of humanity where the strings of camels and horses from the North load and unload. All the nationalities of Central Asia may be found there, and most of the folk of India proper. Balkh and Bokhara there meet Bengal and Bombay, and try to draw eye-teeth. You can buy ponies, turquoises, Persian pussy-cats, saddle-bags, fat-tailed sheep and musk in the Kumharsen Serai, and get many strange things for nothing. In the afternoon I went down there to see whether my friends intended to keep their word or were lying about drunk.

A priest attired in fragments of ribbons and rags stalked up to me, gravely twisting a child's paper whirligig. Behind him was his servant bending under the load of a crate of mud toys. The two were loading up two camels, and the inhabitants of the Serai watched them with shrieks of laughter.

"The priest is mad," said a horse-dealer to me. "He is going up to Kabul to sell toys to the Amir. He will either be raised to honor or have his head cut off. He came in here this morning and has been behaving madly ever since."

"The witless are under the protection of God," stammered a flat-cheeked Usbeg in broken Hindi. "They foretell future events."

"Would they could have foretold that my caravan would have been cut up by the Shinwaris almost within shadow of the Pass!" grunted the Eusufzai agent of a Rajputana trading-house whose goods had been feloniously diverted into the hands of other robbers just across the Border, and whose misfortunes were the laughing-stock of the bazar. "Ohé, priest, whence come you and whither do you go?"

"From Roum have I come," shouted the priest, waving his whirl-igig; "from Roum, blown by the breath of a hundred devils across the sea! O thieves, robbers, liars, the blessing of Pir Khan on pigs, dogs and perjurers! Who will take the Protected of God to the North to sell charms that are never still to the Amir? The camels shall not gall, the sons shall not fall sick, and the wives shall remain faithful while they are away, of the men who give me place in their caravan. Who will assist me to slipper the King of the Roos with a golden slipper with a silver heel? The protection of Pir Khan be upon his labors!" He spread out the skirts of his gaberdine and pirouetted between the lines of tethered horses.

"There starts a caravan from Peshawar to Kabul in twenty days, *Huzrut,*" said the Eusufzai trader. "My camels go therewith. Do thou also go and bring us good-luck."

"I will go even now!" shouted the priest. "I will depart upon my winged camels, and be at Peshawar in a day! Ho! Hazar Mir Khan," he yelled to his servant, "drive out the camels, but let me first mount my own."

He leaped on the back of his beast as it knelt, and, turning round to me, cried: "Come thou also, Sahib, a little along the road, and I will sell thee a charm—an amulet that shall make thee King of Kafiristan."

Then the light broke upon me, and I followed the two camels out of the Serai till we reached open road and the priest halted.

"What d' you think o' that?" said he in English. "Carnehan can't talk their patter, so I've made him my servant. He makes a handsome servant. 'Tisn't for nothing that I've been knocking about the country for fourteen years. Didn't I do that talk neat? We'll hitch on to a caravan at Peshawar till we get to Jagdallak, and then we'll see if we can get donkeys for our camels, and strike into Kafiristan. Whirligigs for the Amir, O Lor! Put your hand under the camel-bags and tell me what you feel."

I felt the butt of a Martini, and another and another.

"Twenty of 'em," said Dravot placidly. "Twenty of 'em, and ammunition to correspond, under the whirligigs and the mud dolls."

"Heaven help you if you are caught with those things!" I said. "A Martini is worth her weight in silver among the Pathans."

"Fifteen hundred rupees of capital—every rupee we could beg, borrow, or steal—are invested on these two camels," said Dravot. "We won't get caught. We're going through the Khaiber with a regular caravan. Who'd touch a poor mad priest?"

"Have you got everything you want?" I asked, overcome with astonishment.

"Not yet, but we shall soon. Give us a memento of your kindness, *Brother*. You did me a service yesterday, and that time in Marwar. Half my Kingdom shall you have, as the saying is." I slipped a small charm compass from my watch-chain and handed it up to the priest.

"Good-by," said Dravot, giving me his hand cautiously. "It's the last time we'll shake hands with an Englishman these many days. Shake hands with him, Carnehan," he cried, as the second camel passed me.

Carnehan leaned down and shook hands. Then the camels passed away along the dusty road, and I was left alone to wonder. My eye could detect no failure in the disguises. The scene in the Serai attested that they were complete to the native mind. There was just the chance, therefore, that Carnehan and Dravot would be able to wander through Afghanistan without detection. But, beyond, they would find death, certain and awful death.

Ten days later a native friend of mine, giving me the news of the day from Peshawar, wound up his letter with: "There has been much laughter here on account of a certain mad priest who is going in his estimation to sell petty gauds and insignificant trinkets which he ascribes as great charms to H. H. the Amir of Bokhara. He passed through Peshawar and associated himself to the Second Summer caravan that goes to Kabul. The merchants are pleased because through superstition they imagine that such mad fellows bring goodfortune."

The two, then, were beyond the Border. I would have prayed for them, but that night a real King died in Europe, and demanded an obituary notice.

The wheel of the world swings through the same phases again and again. Summer passed and winter thereafter, and came and passed again. The daily paper continued and I with it, and upon the third summer there fell a hot night, a night-issue, and a strained waiting for something to be telegraphed from the other side of the world, exactly as had happened before. A few great men had died in the past two years, the machines worked with more clatter, and some of the trees in the Office garden were a few feet taller. But that was all the difference.

I passed over to the press-room, and went through just such a scene as I have already described. The nervous tension was stronger than it had been two years before, and I felt the heat more acutely. At three o'clock I cried "print off," and turned to go, when there crept to my chair what was left of a man. He was bent into a circle, his head was sunk between his shoulders, and he moved his feet one over the other like a bear. I could hardly see whether he walked or crawled—this rag-wrapped, whining cripple who addressed me by name, crying that he was come back. "Can you give me a drink?" he whimpered. "For the Lord's sake, give me a drink!"

I went back to the office, the man following with groans of pain, and I turned up the lamp.

"Don't you know me?" he gasped, dropping into a chair, and he turned his drawn face, surmounted by a shock of gray hair, to the light.

I looked at him intently. Once before had I seen eyebrows that met over the nose in an inch-broad black band, but for the life of me I could not tell where.

"I don't know you," I said, handing him the whisky. "What can I do for you?"

He took a gulp of the spirit raw, and shivered in spite of the suffocating heat.

"I've come back," he repeated; "and I was the King of Kafiristan—me and Dravot—crowned Kings we was! In this office we settled it—you setting there and giving us the books. I am Peachey—Peachey Taliaferro Carnehan, and you've been setting here ever since—O Lord!"

I was more than a little astonished and expressed my feelings accordingly.

"It's true," said Carnehan, with a dry cackle, nursing his feet, which were wrapped in rags. "True as gospel. Kings we were, with crowns upon our heads—me and Dravot—poor Dan—oh, poor, poor Dan, that would never take advice, not though I begged of him!"

"Take the whisky," I said, "and take your own time. Tell me all you can recollect of everything from beginning to end. You got across the border on your camels, Dravot dressed as a mad priest, and you his servant. Do you remember that?"

"I ain't mad—yet, but I shall be that way soon. Of course I remember. Keep looking at me, or maybe my words will go all to pieces. Keep looking at me in my eyes and don't say anything."

I leaned forward and looked into his face as steadily as I could. He dropped one hand upon the table and I grasped it by the wrist. It was twisted like a bird's claw, and upon the back was a ragged, red, diamond-shaped scar.

"No, don't look there. Look at *me*," said Carnehan.

"That comes afterwards, but for the Lord's sake don't distrack me. We left with that caravan, me and Dravot playing all sorts of antics to amuse the people we were with. Dravot used to make us laugh in the evening when all the people was cooking their dinners—cooking their dinners, and . . . . what did they do then? They lit little fires with sparks that went into Dravot's beard, and we all laughed—fit to die. Litle red fires they was, going into Dravot's big red beard—so funny." His eyes left mine and he smiled foolishly.

"You went as far as Jagdallak with that caravan," I said at a venture, "after you had lit those fires. To Jagdallak, where you turned off to try to get into Kafiristan."

"No, we didn't neither. What are you talking about? We turned off before Jagdallak, because we heard the roads was good. But they wasn't good enough for our two camels—mine and Dravot's. When we left the caravan Dravot took off all his clothes and mine too, and said we would be heathen, because the Kafirs didn't allow

Mohammedans to talk to them. So we dressed betwixt and between, and such a sight as Daniel Dravot I never saw yet nor expect to see again. He burned half his beard, and slung a sheepskin over his shoulder, and shaved his head into patterns. He shaved mine, too, and made me wear outrageous things to look like a heathen. That was in a most mountainous country, and our camels couldn't go along any more because of the mountains. They were tall and black, and coming home I saw them fight like wild goats—there are lots of goats in Kafiristan. And these mountains, they never keep still, no more than the goats. Always fighting they are, and don't let you sleep at night."

"Take some more whisky," I said very slowly. "What did you and Daniel Dravot do when the camels could go no further because of the rough roads that led into Kafiristan?"

"What did which do? There was a party called Peachey Taliaferro Carnehan that was with Dravot. Shall I tell you about him? He died out there in the cold. Slap from the bridge fell old Peachey, turning and twisting in the air like a penny whirligig that you can sell to the Amir.—No; they was two for three ha'pence, those whirligigs, or I am much mistaken and woful sore. And then these camels were no use, and Peachey said to Dravot: 'For the Lord's sake, let's get out of this before our heads are chopped off,' and with that they killed the camels all among the mountains, not having anything in particular to eat, but first they took off the boxes with the guns and the ammunition, till two men came along driving four mules. Dravot up and dances in front of them, singing: 'Sell me four mules.' Says the first man: 'If you are rich enough to buy you are rich enough to rob'; but before ever he could put his hand to his knife Dravot breaks his neck over his knee, and the other party runs away. So Carnehan loaded the mules with the rifles that was taken off the camels, and together we starts forward into those bitter cold mountainous parts, and never a road broader than the back of your hand."

He paused for a moment, while I asked him if he could remember the nature of the country through which he had journeyed.

"I am telling you as straight as I can, but my head isn't as good as it might be. They drove nails through it to make me hear better how Dravot died. The country was mountainous and the mules were most contrary, and the inhabitants was dispersed and solitary. They went up and up, and down and down, and that other party, Carnehan, was imploring of Dravot not to sing and whistle so loud, for fear of bringing down the tremenjus avalanches. But Dravot says that if a

King couldn't sing it wasn't worth being King, and whacked the mules over the rump, and never took no heed for ten cold days. We came to a big level valley all among the mountains, and the mules were near dead, so we killed them, not having anything in special for them or us to eat. We sat upon the boxes, and played odd and even with the cartridges that was jolted out.

"Then ten men with bows and arrows ran down that valley chasing twenty men with bows and arrows, and the row was tremenjus. They was fair men—fairer than you or me—with yellow hair and remarkable well built. Says Dravot, unpacking the guns: 'This is the beginning of the business. We'll fight for the ten men,' and with that he fires two rifles at the twenty men, and drops one of them at two hundred yards from the rock where we was sitting. The other men began to run, but Carnehan and Dravot sits on the boxes picking them off at all ranges, up and down the valley. Then we goes up to the ten men that had run across the snow, too, and they fires a footy little arrow at us. Dravot he shoots above their heads and they all falls down flat. Then he walks over them and kicks them, and then he lifts them up and shakes hands all round to make them friendly like. He calls them and gives them the boxes to carry, and waves his hand for all the world as though he was King already. They take the boxes and him across the valley and up the hill into a pine wood on the top, where there was half a dozen big stone idols. Dravot he goes to the biggest—a fellow they call Imbra—and lays a rifle and a cartridge at his feet, rubbing his nose respectful with his own nose, patting him on the head, and saluting in front of it. He turns round to the men and nods his head, and says, 'That's all right. I'm in the know, too, and all these old jim-jams are my friends.' Then he opens his mouth and points down it, and when the first man brings him food, he says—'No'; and when the second man brings him food, he says—'No'; but when one of the old priests and the boss of the village brings him food, he says—'Yes'; very haughty, and eats it slow. That was how we came to our first village, without any trouble, just as though we had tumbled from the skies. But we tumbled from one of those damned rope-bridges, you see, and you couldn't expect a man to laugh much after that."

"Take some more whisky and go on," I said. "That was the first village you came into. How did you get to be King?"

"I wasn't King," said Carnehan. "Dravot he was the King, and a handsome man he looked with the gold crown on his head and all. Him and the other party stayed in that village, and every morning

Dravot sat by the side of old Imbra, and the people came and worshipped. That was Dravot's order. Then a lot of men came into the valley, and Carnehan and Dravot picks them off with the rifles before they knew where they was, and runs down into the valley and up again the other side, and finds another village, same as the first one, and the people all falls down flat on their faces, and Dravo, says, 'Now what is the trouble between you two villages?' and the people points to a woman, as fair as you or me, that was carried off, and Dravot takes her back to the first village and counts up the dead—eight there was. For each dead man Dravot pours a little milk on the ground and waves his arms like a whirligig and 'That's all right,' says he. Then he and Carnehan takes the big boss of each village by the arm and walks them down into the valley, and shows them how to scratch a line with a spear right down the valley, and gives each a sod of turf from both sides o' the line. Then all the people comes down and shouts like the Devil and all, and Dravot says, 'Go and dig the land, and be fruitful and multiply,' which they did, though they didn't understand. Then we asks the names of things in their lingo—bread and water and fire and idols and such, and Dravot leads the priest of each village up to the idol, and says he must sit there and judge the people, and if anything goes wrong he is to be shot.

"Next week they was all turning up the land in the valley as quiet as bees and much prettier, and the priests heard all the complaints and told Dravot in dumb show what it was about. 'That's just the beginning,' says Dravot. 'They think we're Gods.' He and Carnehan picks out twenty good men and shows them how to click off a rifle and form fours, and advance in line, and they was very pleased to do so, and clever to see the hang of it. Then he takes out his pipe and his baccy-pouch and leaves one at one village and one at the other, and off we two goes to see what was to be done in the next valley. That was all rock, and there was a little village there, and Carnehan says,—'Send 'em to the old valley to plant,' and takes 'em there and gives 'em some land that wasn't took before. They were a poor lot, and we blooded 'em with a kid before letting 'em into the new Kingdom. That was to impress the people, and then they settled down quiet, and Carnehan went back to Dravot who had got into another valley, all snow and ice and most mountainous. There was no people there and the Army got afraid, so Dravot shoots one of them, and goes on till he finds some people in a village, and the Army explains that unless the people wants to be killed they had better not shoot their little matchlocks; for they had matchlocks. We makes friends with the priest and I stays there alone with two of the Army, teaching the men how to drill, and a thundering big Chief comes across the snow with kettle-drums and horns twanging, because he heard there was a new God kicking about. Carnehan sights for the brown of the men half a mile across the snow and wings one of them. Then he sends a message to the Chief that, unless he wished to be killed, he must come and shake hands with me and leave his arms behind. The Chief comes alone first, and Carnehan shakes hands with him and whirls his arms about same as Dravot used, and very much surprised that Chief was, and strokes my eyebrows. Then Carnehan goes alone to the Chief and asks him in dumb show if he had an enemy he hated. 'I have,' says the Chief. So Carnehan weeds out the pick of his men, and sets the two of the Army to show them drill and at the end of two weeks the men can maneuver about as well as Volunteers. So he marches with the Chief to a great big plain on the top of a mountain, and the Chief's men rushes into a village and takes it; we three Martinis firing into the brown of the enemy. So we took that village too, and I gives the Chief a rag from my coat, and says, 'Occupy till I come,' which was scriptural. By way of a reminder, when me and the Army was eighteen hundred yards away, I drops a bullet near him standing on the snow, and all the people falls flat on their faces. Then I sends a letter to Dravot, wherever he be by land or by sea."

At the risk of throwing the creature out of train I interrupted, "How could you write a letter up yonder?"

"The letter? Oh! The letter! Keep looking at me between the eyes, please. It was a string-talk letter, that we'd learned the way of it from a blind beggar in the Punjab."

I remember that there had once come to the office a blind man with a knotted twig and a piece of string which he wound round the twig according to some cypher of his own. He could, after the lapse of days or hours, repeat the sentence which he had reeled up. He had reduced the alphabet to eleven primitive sounds; and tried to teach me his method, but failed.

"I sent that letter to Dravot," said Carnehan; "and told him to come back because this Kingdom was growing too big for me to handle, and then I struck for the first valley, to see how the priests were working. They called the village we took along with the Chief, Bashkai, and the first village we took Er-Heb. The priests at Er-Heb was doing all right, but they had a lot of pending cases about land to show me, and some men from another village had been firing arrows at night. I went out and looked for that village and fired four rounds at it from a thousand yards. That used all the cartridges I cared to spend, and I waited for Dravot, who had been away two or three months, and I kept my people quiet.

"One morning I heard the devil's own noise of drums and horns, and Dan Dravot marches down the hill with his Army and a tail of hundreds of men, and, which was the most amazing—a great gold crown on his head. 'My Gord, Carnehan,' says Daniel, 'this is a tremenjus business, and we've got the whole country as far as it's worth having. I am the son of Alexander by Queen Semiramis, and you're my younger brother and a God too! It's the biggest thing we've ever seen. I've been marching and fighting for six weeks with the Army, and every footy little village for fifty miles has come in rejoiceful; and more than that, I've got the key of the whole show, as you'll see, and I've got a crown for you! I told 'em to make two of 'em at a place called Shu, where the gold lies in the rock like suet in mutton. Gold I've seen, and turquoise I've kicked out of the cliffs, and there's garnets in the sands of the river, and here's a chunk of amber that a man brought me. Call up all the priests and, here, take your crown.'

"One of the men opens a black hair bag and I slips the crown on. It was too small and too heavy, but I wore it for the glory. Hammered gold it was—five-pound weight, like a hoop of a barrel.

"'Peachey,' says Dravot, 'we don't want to fight no more. The Craft's the trick, so help me!' and he brings forward that same Chief that I left at Bashkai—Billy Fish we called him afterwards, because he was so like Billy Fish that drove the big tank-engine at Mach on the Bolan in the old days. 'Shake hands with him,' says Dravot, and I shook hands and nearly dropped, for Billy Fish gave me the Grip. I said nothing, but tried him with the Fellow Craft Grip. He answers all right, and I tried the Master's Grip, but that was a slip. 'A Fellow Craft he is!' I says to Dan. 'Does he know the word?' 'He does,' says Dan, 'and all the priests know. It's a miracle! The Chiefs and the priests can work a Fellow Craft Lodge in a way that's very like ours, and they've cut the marks on the rocks, but they don't know the Third Degree, and they've come to find out. It's Gord's Truth. I've known these long years that the Afghans knew up to the Fellow Craft Degree, but this is a miracle. A God and a Grand-Master of the Craft am I, and a Lodge in the Third Degree I will open, and we'll raise the head priests and the Chiefs of the villages.'

" 'It's against all the law,' I says, 'holding a Lodge without warrant from any one; and we never held office in any Lodge.'

" 'It's a master-stroke of policy,' says Dravot. 'It means running the country as easy as a four-wheeled bogy on a down grade. We can't stop to inquire now, or they'll turn against us. I've forty Chiefs at my heel, and passed and raised according to their merit they shall be. Billet these men on the villages, and see that we run up a Lodge of some kind. The temple of Imbra will do for the Lodge room. The women must make aprons as you show them. I'll hold a levee of Chiefs to-night and Lodge to-morrow.'

"I was fair run off my legs, but I wasn't such a fool as not to see what a pull this Craft business gave us. I showed the priests' families how to make aprons of the degrees, but for Dravot's apron the blue border and marks was made of turquoise lumps on white hide, not cloth. We took a great square stone in the temple for the Master's chair, and little stones for the officers' chairs, and painted the black pavement with white squares, and did what we could to make things regular.

"At the levee which was held that night on the hillside with big bonfires, Dravot gives out that him and me were Gods and sons of Alexander, and Past Grand-Masters in the Craft, and was come to make Kafiristan a country where every man should eat in peace and drink in quiet, and specially obey us. Then the Chiefs come round to shake hands, and they was so hairy and white and fair it was just shaking hands with old friends. We gave them names according as they was like men we had known in India—Billy Fish, Holly Dilworth, Pikky Kergan that was Bazar-master when I was at Mhow, and so on and so on.

"*The* most amazing miracle was at Lodge next night. One of the old priests was watching us continuous, and I felt uneasy, for I knew we'd have to fudge the Ritual, and I didn't know what the men knew. The old priest was a stranger come in from beyond the village of Bashkai. The minute Dravot puts on the Master's apron that the girls had made for him, the priest fetches a whoop and a howl, and tries to overturn the stone that Dravot was sitting on. 'It's all up now,' I says. 'That comes of meddling with the Craft without warrant!' Dravot never winked an eye, not when ten priests took and tilted over the Grand-Master's chair—which was to say the stone of Imbra. The priest begins rubbing the bottom one of it to clear away the black dirt, and presently he shows all the other priests the Master's Mark, same as was on Dravot's apron, cut into the stone. Not even the priests of the temple of Imbra knew it was there. The old chap falls flat on his face at Dravot's feet and kisses 'em. 'Luck again,' says Dravot, across the Lodge to me, 'they say it's the missing Mark that no one could understand the why of. We're more than safe now.' Then he bangs the butt of his gun for a gavel and says: 'By virtue of the authority vested in me by my own right hand and the help of Peachey, I declare myself Grand-Master of all Freemasonry in Kafiristan in this the Mother Lodge o' the country, and King of Kafiristan equally with Peachey!' At that he puts on his crown and I puts on mine—I was doing Senior Warden—and we opens the Lodge in most ample form. It was an amazing miracle! The priests moved in Lodge through the first two degrees almost without telling, as if the memory was coming back to them. After that Peachey and Dravot raised such as was worthy—high priests and Chiefs of far-off villages. Billy Fish was the first, and I can tell you we scared the soul out of him. It was not in any way according to Ritual, but it served our turn. We didn't raise more than ten of the biggest men because we didn't want to make the Degree common. And they was clamoring to be raised.

" 'In another six months,' says Dravot, 'we'll hold another Communication and see how you are working.' Then he asks them about their villages, and learns that they was fighting one against the other and were fair sick and tired of it. And when they wasn't doing that they was fighting with the Mohammedans. 'You can fight those when they come into our country,' says Dravot. 'Tell off every tenth man of your tribes for a Frontier guard, and send two hundred at a time to this valley to be drilled. Nobody is going to be shot or speared any more so long as he does well, and I know that you won't cheat me because you're white people—sons of Alexander—and not like common, black Mohammedans. You are *my* people, and by God,' says he, running off into English at the end—'I'll make a damned fine Nation of you, or I'll die in the making!'

"I can't tell all we did for the next six months, because Dravot did a lot I couldn't see the hang of, and he learned their lingo in a way I never could. My work was to help the people plough, and now and again go out with some of the Army and see what the other villages were doing, and make 'em throw rope bridges across the ravines which cut up the country horrid. Dravot was very kind to me, but when he walked up and down in the pine wood pulling that bloody red beard of his with both fists I knew he was thinking plans I could not advise him about and I just waited for orders.

"But Dravot never showed me disrespect before the people. They were afraid of me and the Army, but they loved Dan. He was the best of friends with the priests and the Chiefs; but any one could come across the hills with a complaint and Dravot would hear him out fair, and call four priests together and say what was to be done. He used to call in Billy Fish from Bashkai, and Pikky Kergen from Shu, and an old Chief we called Kefuzelum—it was like enough to his real name—and hold councils with 'em when there was any fighting to be done in small villages. That was his Council of War, and the four priests of Bashkai, Shu, Khawak and Madora was his Privy Council. Between the lot of 'em they sent me, with forty men and twenty rifles, and sixty men carrying turquoises, into the Ghorband country to buy those hand-made Martini rifles that come out of the Amir's workshops at Kabul, from one of the Amir's Herati regiments that would have sold the very teeth out of their mouths for turquoises.

"I stayed in Ghorband a month, and gave the Governor there the pick of my baskets for hush-money, and bribed the Colonel of the regiment some more, and between the two and the tribes people, we got more than a hundred handmade Martinis, a hundred good Kohat Jezails that'll throw to six hundred yards, and forty man-loads of very bad ammunition for the rifles. I came back with what I had, and distributed 'em among the men that the Chiefs sent in to me to drill. Dravot was too busy to attend to those things, but the old Army that we first made helped me, and we turned out five hundred men that could drill, and two hundred that knew how to hold arms pretty straight. Even those cork-screwed, hand-made guns was a miracle to them. Dravot talked big about powder-shops and factories, walking up and down in the pine wood when the winter was coming on.

" 'I won't make a Nation,' says he. 'I'll make an Empire! These men aren't niggers; they're English! Look at their eyes—look at their mouths. Look at the way they stand up. They sit on chairs in their own houses. They're the Lost Tribes, or something like it, and they've grown to be English. I'll take a census in the spring if the priests don't get frightened. There must be fair two million of 'em in these hills. The villages are full o' little children. The million people—two hundred and fifty thousand fighting men—and all English! They only want the rifles and a little drilling. Two hundred and fifty thousand men, ready to cut in on Russia's right flank when she tries for India! Peachey, man,' he says, chewing his beard in great hunks, 'we shall be Emperors—Emperors of the Earth! Rajah Brooke will be a suckling to us. I'll treat with the Viceroy on equal terms. I'll ask him to send me twelve picked English—twelve that I know of—to help us govern a bit. There's Mackray, Sergeant-pensioner at Segowli—many's the good dinner he's given me, and his wife a pair of trousers. There's Donkin, the Warder of Tounghoo Jail; there's hundreds that I could lay my hands on if I was in India. The Viceroy shall do it for me. I'll send a man through in the spring for those men, and I'll write for a dispensation from the Grand Lodge for what I've done as Grand-Master. That—and all the Sniders that'll be thrown out when the native troops in India take up the Martini. They'll be worn smooth, but they'll do for fighting in these hills. Twelve English, a hundred thousand Sniders run through the Amir's country in driblets—I'd be content with twenty thousand in one year—and we'd be an Empire. When everything was shipshape, I'd hand over the crown—this crown I'm wearing now—to Queen Victoria on my knees, and she'd say: "Rise up, Sir Daniel Dravot." Oh, it's big! It's big, I tell you! But there's so much to be done in every place—Bashkai, Khawak, Shu, and everywhere else.'

" 'What is it?' I says. 'There are no more men coming in to be drilled this autumn. Look at those fat, black clouds. They're bringing the snow.'

" 'It isn't that,' says Daniel, putting his hand very hard on my shoulder; 'and I don't wish to say anything that's against you, for no other living man would have followed me and made me what I am as you have done. You're a first-class Commander-in-Chief, and the people know you; but—it's a big country, and somehow you can't help me, Peachey, in the way I want to be helped.'

" 'Go to your blasted priests, then!' I said, and I was sorry when I made that remark, but it did hurt me sore to find Daniel talking so superior when I'd drilled all the men, and done all he told me.

" 'Don't let's quarrel, Peachey,' says Daniel without cursing. 'You're a King too, and the half of this Kingdom is yours; but can't you see, Peachey, we want cleverer men than us now—three or four of 'em, that we can scatter about for our Deputies. It's a huge great State, and I can't always tell the right thing to do, and I haven't time for all I want to do, and here's the winter coming on and all.' He put half his beard into his mouth, and it was as red as the gold of his crown.

" 'I'm sorry, Daniel,' says I. 'I've done all I could. I've drilled the men and shown the people how to stack their oats better; and I've brought in those tinware rifles from Ghorband—but I know what you're driving at. I take it Kings always feel oppressed that way.'

"'There's another thing, too,' says Dravot, walking up and down. 'The winter's coming and these people won't be giving much trouble, and if they do we can't move about. I want a wife.'

"'For Gord's sake leave the women alone!' I says. 'We've both got all the work we can, though I *am* a fool. Remember the Contrack and keep clear o' women.'

"'The Contrack only lasted till such time as we was Kings; and Kings we have been these months past,' says Dravot, weighing his crown in his hand. 'You go get a wife too, Peachy, a nice, strappin', plump girl that'll keep you warm in the winter. They're prettier than English girls, and we can take the pick of 'em. Boil 'em once or twice in hot water and they'll come as fair as chicken and ham.'

"'Don't tempt me!' I says. 'I will not have any dealings with a woman not till we are a dam' side more settled than we are now. I've been doing the work o' two men, and you've been doing the work o' three. Let's lie off a bit, and see if we can get some better tobacco from Afghan country and run in some good liquor; but no women.'

"'Who's talking o' *women*?' says Dravot. 'I said *wife*—a Queen to breed a King's son for the King. A Queen out of the strongest tribe, that'll make them your blood-brothers, and that'll lie by your side and tell you all the people thinks about you and their own affairs. That's what I want.'

"'Do you remember that Bengali woman I kept at Mogul Serai when I was a plate layer?' says I. 'A fat lot o' good she was to me. She taught me the lingo and one or two other things; but what happened? She ran away with the Station Master's servant and half my month's pay. Then she turned up at Dadur Junction in tow of a half-caste, and had the impidence to say I was her husband—all among the drivers in the running-shed!'

"'We've done with that,' says Dravot. 'These women are whiter than you or me, and a Queen I will have for the winter months.'

"'For the last time o' asking, Dan, do *not*,' I says. 'It'll only bring us harm. The Bible says that Kings ain't to waste their strength on women, 'specially when they've got a new raw Kingdom to work over.'

"'For the last time of answering I will,' says Dravot, and he went away through the pine trees looking like a big red devil. The low sun hit his crown and beard on one side, and the two blazed like hot coals.

"But getting a wife was not as easy as Dan thought. He put it before the Council, and there was no answer till Billy Fish said that he'd better ask the girls. Dravot damned them all round. 'What's wrong with me?' he shouts, standing by the idol Imbra. 'Am I a dog or am I not enough of a man for your wenches? Haven't I put the shadow of my hand over this country? Who stopped the last Afghan raid?' It was me really, but Dravot was too angry to remember. 'Who bought your guns? Who repaired the bridges? Who's the Grand-Master of the sign cut in the stone?' and he thumped his hand on the block that he used to sit on in Lodge, and at Council, which opened like Lodge always. Billy Fish said nothing and no more did the others. 'Keep your hair on, Dan,' said I; 'and ask the girls. That's how it's done at Home, and these people are quite English.'

" 'The marriage of the King is a matter of State,' says Dan, in a white-hot rage, for he could feel, I hope, that he was going against his better mind. He walked out of the Council room, and the others sat still, looking at the ground.

" 'Billy Fish,' says I to the Chief of the Bashkai, 'what's the difficulty here? A straight answer to a true friend.' 'You know,' says Billy Fish. 'How should a man tell you, who know everything? How can daughters of men marry Gods or Devils? It's not proper.'

"I remembered something like that in the Bible; but if, after seeing us as long as they had, they still believed we were Gods, it wasn't for me to undeceive them.

" 'A God can do anything,' says I. 'If the King is fond of a girl he'll not let her die.' 'She'll have to,' said Billy Fish. 'There are all sorts of Gods and Devils in these mountains, and now and again a girl marries one of them and isn't seen any more. Besides, you two know the Mark cut in the stone. Only the Gods know that. We thought you were men till you showed the sign of the Master.'

"I wished then that we had explained about the loss of the genuine secrets of a Master-Mason at the first go-off; but I said nothing. All that night there was a blowing of horns in a little dark temple halfway down the hill, and I heard a girl crying fit to die. One of the priests told us that she was being prepared to marry the King.

" 'I'll have no nonsense of that kind,' says Dan. 'I don't want to interfere with your customs, but I'll take my own wife.' 'The girl's a little bit afraid,' says the priest. 'She thinks she's going to die, and they are a-heartening her up down in the temple.'

" 'Hearten her very tender, then,' says Dravot, 'or I'll hearten you with the butt of a gun so that you'll never want to be heartened again.' He licked his lips, did Dan, and stayed up walking about more than half the night, thinking of the wife that he was going to get in the morning. I wasn't any means comfortable, for I knew that dealings with a woman in foreign parts, though you was a crowned King twenty times over, could not but be risky. I got up very early in the morning while Dravot was asleep, and I saw the priests talking together in whispers, and the Chiefs talking together, too, and they looked at me out of the corners of their eyes.

" 'What is up, Fish?' I says to the Bashkai man, who was wrapped up in his furs and looking splendid to behold.

" 'I can't rightly say,' says he; 'but if you can induce the King to drop all this nonsense about marriage you'll be doing him and me and yourself a great service.'

" 'That I do believe,' says I. 'But sure, you know, Billy, as well as me, having fought against and for us, that the King and me are nothing more than two of the finest men that God Almighty ever made. Nothing more, I do assure you.'

" 'That may be,' says Billy Fish, 'and yet I should be sorry if it was.' He sinks his head upon his great fur coat for a minute and thinks. 'King,' says he, 'be you man or God or Devil, I'll stick by you to-day. I have twenty of my men with me, and they will follow me. We'll go to Bashkai until the storm blows over.'

"A little snow had fallen in the night, and everything was white except the greasy fat clouds that blew down and down from the north. Dravot came out with his crown on his head, swinging his arms and stamping his feet, and looking more pleased than Punch.

" 'For the last time drop it, Dan,' says I in a whisper. 'Billy Fish here says that there will be a row.'

" 'A row among my people!' says Dravot. 'Not much. Peachey, you're a fool not to get a wife too. Where's the girl?' says he with a voice as loud as the braying of a jackass. 'Call up all the Chiefs and priests, and let the Emperor see if his wife suits him.'

"There was no need to call any one. They were all there leaning on their guns and spears round the clearing in the centre of the pine wood. A deputation of priests went down to the little temple to bring up the girl, and the horns blew fit to wake the dead. Billy Fish saunters round and gets as close to Daniel as he could, and behind him stood his twenty men with matchlocks. Not a man of them under six feet. I was next to Dravot, and behind me was twenty men of the regular

Army. Up comes the girl, and a strapping wench she was, covered with silver and turquoises, but white as death, and looking back every minute at the priests.

" 'She'll do,' said Dan, looking her over. 'What's to be afraid of, lass? Come and kiss me.' He puts his arm round her. She shuts her eyes, gives a bit of a squeak, and down goes her face in the side of Dan's flaming red beard.

" 'The slut's bitten me!' says he, clapping his hand to his neck; and sure enough his hand was red with blood. Billy Fish and two of his matchlock-men catches hold of Dan by the shoulders and drags him into the Bashkai lot, while the priests howls in their lingo, 'Neither God nor Devil but a man!' I was all taken aback, for a priest cut at me in front, and the Army began firing into the Bashkai men.

" 'God A-mighty!' says Dan. 'What is the meaning o' this?'

" 'Come back! Come away!' says Billy Fish. 'Ruin and Mutiny is the matter. We'll break for Bashkai if we can.'

"I tried to give some sort of orders to my men—the men o' the regular Army—but it was no use, so I fired into the brown of 'em with an English Martini and drilled three beggars in a line. The valley was full of shouting, howling creatures, and every soul was shrieking, 'Not a God nor a Devil but only a man!' The Bashkai troops stuck to Billy Fish all they were worth, but their matchlocks wasn't half as good as the Kabul breech-loaders, and four of them dropped. Dan was bellowing like a bull, for he was very wrathy; and Billy Fish had a hard job to prevent him running out at the crowd.

" 'We can't stand,' says Billy Fish. 'Make a run for it down the valley! The whole place is against us.' The matchlock-men ran, and we went down the valley in spite of Dravot's protestations. He was swearing horribly and crying out that he was a King. The priests rolled great stones on us, and the regular army fired hard, and there wasn't more than six men, not counting Dan, Billy Fish and Me that came down to the bottom of the valley alive.

"Then they stopped firing and the horns in the temple blew again. 'Come away—for Gord's sake come away!' says Billy Fish. 'They'll send runners out to all the villages before ever we get to Bashkai. I can protect you there, but I can't do anything now.'

"My own notion is that Dan began to go mad in his head from that hour. He stared up and down like a stuck pig. Then he was all for walking back alone and killing the priests with his bare hands, which he could have done. 'An Emperor am I,' says Daniel, 'and next year I shall be a Knight of the Queen.'

"'All right, Dan,' says I; 'but come along now while there's time.'

"'It's your fault,' says he, 'for not looking after your Army better. There was mutiny in the midst, and you didn't know—you damned engine-driving, plate-laying, missionaries'-pass hunting hound!' He sat upon a rock and called me every foul name he could lay tongue to. I was too heartsick to care, though it was all his foolishness that brought the smash.

"'I'm sorry, Dan,' says I, 'but there's no accounting for natives. This business is our Fifty-Seven. Maybe we'll make something out of it yet, when we've got back to Bashkai.'

"'Let's get to Bashkai, then,' says Dan, 'and by God, when I come back here again I'll sweep the valley so there isn't a bug in a blanket left!'

"We walked all that day, and all that night Dan was stumping up and down on the snow, chewing his beard and muttering to himself.

"'There's no hope o' getting clear,' said Billy Fish. 'The priests will have sent runners to the villages to say that you are only men. Why didn't you stick on as Gods till things was more settled? I'm a dead man,' says Billy Fish, and he throws himself down on the snow and begins to pray to his Gods.

"Next morning we was in a cruel bad country—all up and down, no level ground at all, and no food either. The six Bashkai men looked at Billy Fish hungry-wise as if they wanted to ask something, but they said never a word. At noon we came to the top of a flat mountain all covered with snow, and when we climbed up into it, behold, there was an Army in position waiting in the middle!

"'The runners have been very quick,' says Billy Fish, with a little bit of a laugh. 'They are waiting for us.'

"Three or four men began to fire from the enemy's side, and a chance shot took Daniel in the calf of the leg. That brought him to his senses. He looks across the snow at the Army, and sees the rifles that we had brought into the country.

"'We're done for,' says he. 'They are Englishmen, these people—and it's my blasted nonsense that has brought you to this. Get back, Billy Fish, and take your men away; you've done what you could, and now cut for it. Carnehan,' says he, 'shake hands with me and go along with Billy. Maybe they won't kill you. I'll go and meet 'em alone. It's me that did it. Me, the King!'

"'Go!' says I. 'Go to Hell, Dan. I'm with you here. Billy Fish you clear out and we two will meet those folk.'

" 'I'm a Chief,' says Billy Fish quite quiet. 'I stay with you. My men can go.'

"The Bashkai fellows didn't wait for a second word but ran off, and Dan and Me and Billy Fish walked across to where the drums were drumming and the horns were horning. It was cold—awful cold. I've got that cold in the back of my head now. There's a lump of it there."

The punkah-coolies had gone to sleep. Two kerosene lamps were blazing in the office, and the perspiration poured down my face and splashed on the blotter as I leaned forward. Carnehan was shivering, and I feared that his mind might go. I wiped my face, took a fresh grip of the piteously mangled hands and said:—"What happened after that?"

The momentary shift of my eyes had broken the clear current.

"What was you pleased to say?" whined Carnehan. "They took them without any sound. Not a little whisper all along the snow, not though the King knocked down the first man that set hand on him— not though old Peachey fired his last cartridge into the brown of 'em. Not a single solitary sound did those swines make. They just closed up tight, and I tell you their furs stunk. There was a man called Billy Fish, a good friend of us all, and they cut his throat, Sir, then and there, like a pig; and the King kicks up the bloody snow and says:—'We've had a dashed fine run for our money. What's coming next?' But Peachey, Peachey Taliaferro, I tell you, Sir, in confidence as betwixt two friends, he lost his head, Sir. No, he didn't either. The King lost his head, so he did, all along o' one of those cunning rope-bridges. Kindly let me have the paper-cutter, Sir. It tilted this way. They marched him a mile across that snow to a rope bridge over a ravine with a river at the bottom. You may have seen such. They prodded him behind like an ox. 'Damn your eyes!' says the King. 'D'you suppose I can't die like a gentleman?' He turns to Peachey—Peachey that was crying like a child. 'I've brought you to this, Peachey,' says he. 'Brought you out of your happy life to be killed in Kafiristan, where you was late Commander-in-Chief of the Emperor's forces. Say you forgive me, Peachey.' 'I do,' says Peachey. 'Fully and freely do I forgive you, Dan.' 'Shake hands, Peachey,' says he. 'I'm going now.' Out he goes, looking neither right nor left, and when he was plumb in the middle of those dizzy dancing ropes, 'Cut, you beggars,' he shouts; and they cut, and old Dan fell, turning round and round and round, twenty thousand miles, for he took half an hour to fall till he struck the water, and I could see his body caught on a rock with the gold crown close beside.

"But do you know what they did to Peachey between two pine trees? They crucified him, Sir, as Peachey's hands will show. They used wooden pegs for his hands and his feet; and he didn't die. He hung there and screamed; and they took him down next day and said it was a miracle that he wasn't dead. They took him down—poor old Peachey that hadn't done them any harm—that hadn't done them any . . ."

He rocked to and fro and wept bitterly, wiping his eyes with the back of his scarred hands and moaning like a child for some ten minutes.

"They was cruel enough to feed him up in the temple, because they said he was more of a God than old Daniel that was a man. Then they turned him out on the snow, and told him to go home; and Peachey came home in about a year, begging along the roads quite safe; for Daniel Dravot he walked before and said: 'Come along, Peachey. It's a big thing we're doing.' The mountains they danced at night, and the mountains they tried to fall on Peachey's head, but Dan he held up his hand and Peachey came along bent double. He never let go of Dan's hand, and he never let go of Dan's head. They gave it to him as a present in the temple, to remind him not to come again, and though the crown was pure gold, and Peachey was starving, never would Peachey sell the same. You knew Dravot, Sir! You knew Right Worshipful Brother Dravot! Look at him now!"

He fumbled in the mass of rags round his bent waist; brought out a black horsehair bag embroidered with silver thread; and shook therefrom onto my table—the dried, withered head of Daniel Dravot! The morning sun that had long been paling the lamps struck the red beard and blind, sunken eyes; struck, too, a heavy circlet of gold studded with raw turquoises, that Carnehan placed tenderly on the battered temples.

"You behold now," said Carnehan, "the Emperor in his habit as he lived—the King of Kafiristan with his crown upon his head. Poor old Daniel that was a monarch once!"

I shuddered, for, in spite of defacements manifold, I recognized the head of the man of Marwar Junction. Carnehan rose to go. I attempted to stop him. He was not fit to walk abroad. "Let me take away the whisky and give me a little money," he gasped. "I was a King once. I'll go to the Deputy Commissioner and ask to set in the Poorhouse till I get my health. No, thank you, I can't wait till you get a carriage for me. I've urgent private affairs—in the south—at Marwar."

He shambled out of the office and departed in the direction of the Deputy Commissioner's house. That day at noon I had occasion to go down the blinding hot Mall, and I saw a crooked man crawling along the white dust of the roadside, his hat in his hand, quavering dolorously after the fashion of street-singers at Home. There was not a soul in sight, and he was out of all possible earshot of the houses. And he sang through his nose, turning his head from right to left:

> "The Son of Man goes forth to war,
>   A golden crown to gain;
> His blood-red banner streams afar—
>   Who follows in his train?"

I waited to hear no more, but put the poor wretch into my carriage and drove him off to the nearest missionary for eventual transfer to the Asylum. He repeated the hymn twice while he was with me, whom he did not in the least recognize, and I left him singing it to the missionary.

Two days later I inquired after his welfare of the Superintendent of the Asylum.

"He was admitted suffering from sunstroke. He died early yesterday morning," said the Superintendent. "Is it true that he was half an hour bareheaded in the sun at midday?"

"Yes," said I; "but do you happen to know if he had anything upon him by any chance when he died?"

"Not to my knowledge," said the Superintendent.

And there the matter rests.